The Law of Miracles

UNIVERSITY OF MASSACHUSETTS PRESS   Amherst and Boston

THE LAW OF
MIRACLES

and other stories

GREGORY BLAKE SMITH

Gregory Blake Smith (signature)

LC 2011003373
ISBN 978-1-55849-900-3

Designed by Sally Nichols
Set in TheSans, and Quaadrat
Printed and bound by BookMobile, Inc.

Library of Congress Cataloging-in-Publication Data

Smith, Gregory Blake.
The law of miracles : short fiction / Gregory Blake Smith.
p. cm.
ISBN 978-1-55849-900-3 (pbk. : alk. paper)
I. Title.
PS3569.M5356L39 2011
813'.54—dc22
                                    2011003373

British Library Cataloguing in Publication data are available.

CONTENTS

The Law of Miracles

Some Moral Problems You Might Like to Ponder of a Winter's Evening, in Front of the Fire, with a Cat on Your Lap

Moral Problem #1:
THE LIBRARIAN IN THE MUD

In this era of the insulted and the reeducated, you have the correct family background to be a model student. Your father was a peasant and your second elder sister was sold as a servant before Liberation. Chairman Mao is your sun and you are his sunflower. When he selects you to go to university, you denounce to your girlish heart the pride you feel.

The things you love are these: Chairman Mao, the Chinese people, the quiet in the Garden of Virtue at the Summer Palace, the plays of Tian Han and *The Lady of the Camellias*, which you have read three times in Chinese. At night, in bed, you sometimes imagine Alfredo coming to you. In these dreams, a yellow Chinese moon hangs in a violet Parisian sky.

At university you no longer take literature classes. The bourgeois subjects have been replaced by "Mao Zedong Thought" and "Skills to Serve the People." In order to pass your course in Applied Marxist Dialectics you must denounce a counter-revolutionary revisionist element. You must follow the Four Methods and speak out freely. It is necessary to demonstrate your revolutionary zeal.

So you make a big-character poster and denounce your department head. He has already been denounced by others so you do not feel responsible. You attend mass criticism sessions. In one your department head is shouted at and slapped. His head has been shaved and there are little streams of blood running down his cheeks from razor cuts. He wears a dunce cap. He wears a tablet slung around his neck. He is made to turn round and round as you shout criticisms at him. You remember how he once spoke to you about Dumas *père* and Dumas *fils*, once about Flaubert. Afterwards you destroy your copy of *The Lady of the Camellias*.

More struggle sessions ensue. You stand with the others in a circle and shout humiliation. But you have run out of criticisms and are repeating yourself. The others look at you. The harsher one is, the more revolutionary. But you are not creative. You repeat yourself. You repeat what others say. The Head sits with neck bowed and sobs. He will not look at you.

And then you make a mistake. As you are copying one of Chairman Mao's sayings for a big-character poster your mind drifts, and instead of writing "Whatever the enemy opposes, we should uphold," you write "Whatever the enemy opposes, we should oppose." It's a silly mistake. It's the sort of thing you do. Sometimes you add the salt twice to recipes for dough. But it is noticed. Your roommate moves out. You begin to see posters about yourself. One says you are guilty of Class Revenge, of being a Rightist. Another says you are the department head's concubine. You come home to your room one day and discover it has been ransacked.

At your struggle session you are made to sit in the middle of a classroom on an upended wastebasket. Someone has drilled a hole in your copy of Tian Han's plays and hung it around your neck. Your head has been shaved. You can feel the blood trickling down behind your ear. When they shout at you sometimes their spittle reaches your face. It is only the first of many such sessions of correction.

In the spring you are sent to the countryside for reeducation. You work in the fields and sleep in a cowshed. You undergo much hardship. It is cold and there is not enough to eat. From time to time you are put in a laundry room with other enemies of the people where you are told to slap one another. If you do not do as you are told you will be taken out and executed. So you slap and are slapped back. Your face turns black and blue and you cannot see out of your right eye. But you are lucky. It is not as bad as it could be.

There is someone here you recognize from the university. A librarian. She sits every morning in a pigsty reading Mao. You try to speak to her but she will not answer. She only bows her head and keeps reading. Her clothes are filthy with mud and urine. You leave her alone but come back the next day. You tell her about your department head and ask her if she knew him. You see tears come to her eyes. On the third day when you tell her you want to cleanse yourself of revisionist ideas, she finally speaks to you. She still will not look at you, but she tells you if you have a favorite book, find a passage you love. Criticize it. It is sure to be wrong.

You are getting thin. A gust of wind could blow you away.

PRESENTLY IN RUINS

The names had the sound of the History Channel: Pearl Harbor, Eniwetok Atoll, Guam. His father had been to each during the Second World War and he, the son, had never known about it. Fifty-one years he'd been alive and to find out who his father had been he had to get like this: drunk, lost, estranged from a minimum of two wives, and a murderer in the eyes of his sister, and maybe the State of Indiana.

He was in a hotel room drinking bourbon and typing bits and pieces of his father's life into Google—the name of the ship he'd served on in the South Pacific, the New England factory he'd worked in for thirty-eight years—zooming the JPEGs to 150% and searching for him in the half-empty bleachers at Braves Field or in the back row of the 1948 Clifton Glee Club. In half a dozen photos he could take this or that man's brushy hair, improvise a nondescript face, and come up with his father. CPO William Pike. Second tenor Willy Pike. He had been there, if not in the photos then in the real world—rooting for the Boston Braves, singing "Shenandoah" in his one suit. That rocky outcrop just off the Eniwetok beach was where he'd maybe sat shirtless in the equatorial sun, had maybe relieved himself there, fretted, wished he was back home in wintry New England. A small, quiet, dreamy man. The Japanese had torpedoed his ship just off the Philippines.

They had grown up, he and his sister, in a sad manufacturing

4

town in the northwestern corner of Connecticut. It had been what his sociology textbook would later call a depressed area, a blue-collar world filled with OK Used Cars and out-of-work older brothers. What lingered in his memory was the feeling of having nothing to do. Hanging around on front porches, on front lawns that were nothing but packed dirt, at night sitting in the television room with his mother and sister watching F Troop while his father worked on his model railroad in the cellar.

It was one of the oddities of his childhood—the presence in the cellar of a 1:87 scale version of the town he was growing up in. Only this was his town circa 1926, a quarter century before he was born, not the Clifton he knew with its closed factories, its empty downtown, its mammoth brass mill turned into a block-square heap of brick like a New England Hiroshima, but the Clifton of his father's boyhood recreated in plaster and epoxy and scale timber. There the American Brass mill had its sawtooth roof intact, the valleys surrounding the town had orchards on their hillsides, kids fishing in the brooks, Model T's motoring up the gravel roads. He had known, even as a child, that his father had lived more in that world than in the real world. That in the real world he was a shy misfit, an object of fun in the factory, of taunting by the neighborhood kids. The son, from his earliest memories, had been ashamed of him.

When, forty years later, he and his sister had come east to help sell the house after their mother died, they had had to break the railroad up, take an axe from off one of the yard-sale tables and bludgeon the layout into a heap of plaster and wood and then haul it out to a dumpster at the side of the road. There had been no other way. His father had stood in his walker on the tarred driveway, his back to the house, watching the clouds sail between the trees while they did it.

———

The USS Shadwell, he learned in between bourbons, had been named after the birthplace ("presently in ruins") of Thomas

Jefferson. There were pictures of it on the website, a big, ungainly thing with a crane used to service amphibious equipment and landing craft. There were links to shops where you could purchase caps, coffee mugs, sweatshirts with "USS Shadwell LSD-15" on them. Also, a link to information about a reunion.

His father had told him—that last night—that the torpedo had been meant for a tanker, but that the convoy had maneuvered and the Shadwell had taken the hit instead of the larger ship. This was not in the official history. Neither were the five hundred men standing on deck in their Mae Wests, waiting for the ship to sink. Or CPO Pike in the midst of them, having to take a leak but not daring to go to the head.

Had there been a need, after all, that last night, to communicate something? To say something about mortality while his son took the bottle of Seconal, the plastic bag, the pantyhose out of his briefcase?

—

After the yard sale, and after closing on the house, they had loaded up a small U-Haul trailer and driven from Connecticut to his sister's in Indiana, spending a night in a motel along Interstate 80 in Pennsylvania. It had been a painful trip for the father. They had had to help him switch back and forth from sitting in the front seat to lying in the back. He was suffering from Paget's disease, a condition in which the bones gradually grow soft and misshapen, and whose prognosis typically includes disintegration of the spine, and compression of the brain as a result of the skull growing malformed. Its chief symptom—the Paget's Disease Support Website had informed the son when he had first logged on three years ago—was pain.

At the Harpswell House the residents dined in a common dining room. They had church services, and bingo, and singing. A hair stylist visited every Tuesday. The aides washed you.

They helped you get dressed, helped you pull your socks on, Velcro your running shoes. They would not, however, cut your toenails. Why, when the son pressed them during one of his semi-monthly visits, was unclear. It had something to do with being an operation in which actual parts of the body were removed. Which was different from washing, or dressing, or brushing teeth.

They had furnished the room with things brought from the old house. A table and two chairs. A lamp. A bookcase. They bought a twenty-five-inch TV, and from a medical supply store a lounger that had a motorized lift mechanism to assist the infirm in standing up. In the bookcase were all his old New England railroad books, and on top of the bookcase a solitary 2-8-2 freight engine. No. 23, a USRA Light Mikado, weathered with oil spots and grime and a touch of rust.

On the TV the Boston Braves, who had become the Milwaukee Braves and were now the Atlanta Braves, were on TBS nearly every night. The whole country could watch them. Their uniforms still had the same script-written *Braves* underlined with the same tomahawk. But it wasn't like walking down Commonwealth Avenue on a May afternoon, paying your 25¢ for a bleacher seat and being one of maybe four thousand men in coats and ties watching a young Casey Stengel manage, watching the lefty Eddie Carnett pitch, Babe Dahlgren bat. Not the same as when you were young, alive, with an eye out for the girls. Maybe it was 50¢.

———

The website mentioned that the *Shadwell*'s gunners had "splashed a Zeke," that it had steered by "trick wheel." What did these things mean? Who was left to tell him?

———

The first time his father tried to kill himself was about a year after he'd moved into the Harpswell House. Jean had called to tell him and the two had spoken in low voices, disbelieving, with long silences. What hung on the line between them was the paradox of their timid, funny, pointless, ineffectual father—the man who when he had first gone to school had been placed with the slow kids in the Opportunity Room—killing himself, taking a bottle of pills, actually *doing* it. (Also, sadly, bitterly—though this might have been true only for the brother—the aptness that he would fail at it.)

They spoke of depression, of the death of their mother, of the pain of the Paget's. They asked each other in hushed tones to imagine the prospect of such pain, the certain knowledge that you would end up bedridden, your bones squeezing you from the inside, your body glowing with pain. The sister had said that: *glowing with pain.*

On the model railroad there had been one figure down in the freight yard, a boy a half-inch tall watching a switch engine making up a milk train. There was a bike propped against his side, a baseball cap on his head. "That's me," the father had said once. He had smiled into the scale distance. That was him as a boy in 1926.

———

His first wife had found his father funny. His second wife had not. He had left his first wife. The second had left him.

———

When they were kids, whenever they went shopping as a family, their father would lag behind, dreamily looking at this thing, that thing, while their mother directed his sister and him in what they were looking for, how much they could spend. When they passed something that was stitched—handbags, suitcases, shaving kits—the father would stop and inspect them, looking to see if the stitching had been done with one of the "Puritan" machines that his company manufactured. He could tell by the type of stitch. When he found one, he touched it with a surprised smile, as if he had found some part of himself functioning properly in the world.

Now, in the hotel room, waiting for the police if the police were going to come, the son typed <puritan sewing Clifton> into Google to see what came up.

Then he typed <'w.w. mertz' 'department store' Clifton>.

Then he typed <'elizabeth skibisky' 'Clifton high school' 'Class of 1969'>.

Why? he wondered. What was he doing?

———

The second time it was with black-market Valium the sister had gotten. They had talked it over on the phone. She knew someone in the plant who knew someone who could get it for her: this, the brother marveled, from the girl who had gone to college in the late sixties and had never to this day done drugs as far as he knew. She wanted him to know that it was just for their father's peace of mind, a kind of insurance policy, something whose presence in the nightstand drawer would calm him when he got scared of the future, of the pain. It was a sort of escape clause, the brother realized, a psychological feint that allowed her to do what was otherwise emotionally off the charts. He, on the other hand, had wanted to know how strong the pills were, would they do the job. She'd answered that the guy in the plant had said it was the really strong stuff. What did that mean? he had asked a little testily, how many milligrams? And there it was in the silence between them, the old antagonism of their childhood: she a little scattered, myopic, trusting; he exacting, demanding, wanting to pin things down, to know what he was about, the future patent attorney. But he had let it go. If she was willing to do this—he could hear the struggle in her voice, the cost, the fear—then never mind the milligrams.

They turned out, by the hospital lab's evaluation, to have been the smallest commercially available dose—2 mg, twenty of them—enough to put their father out for forty-eight hours and to make the six days in the hospital an amnesiac gray, but with no lasting effect. They were monitoring him now, his sister told him over the phone. They would start him on physical therapy in a few days. She had been through an ordeal, she said. She had been terrified the police would ask where the pills came from. That was it for her. She couldn't do any more.

What really annoyed him was that months earlier, after the first attempt, he had gone online and looked up the Hemlock Society, e-mailed them for their literature. There was a right way of doing it. There was even a step-by-step procedure in the booklet, a sidebar with Do's and Don'ts. He had mailed it to her months ago. When he had talked to her on the phone afterwards she'd said it was too ghastly. It was too gruesome: asphyxiation. The elastic bands, the turkey-sized oven bag: she couldn't do it. But she'd asked around and now she knew of a guy in the plant. . . . He should've insisted on the milligrams. Instead he'd let her hide down in the cellar.

(Their mother could have done it, he knew, could have gotten the right stuff, seen to its administration, followed through, closed the deal . . . but she was gone. She was gone and if it was going to get done, he would have to be the one to do it.)

"Four thousand dollars," his father had chuckled when the son finally called. He was speaking of the hospital bill. "Who would think not dying would cost so much?"

———

He searched for <'the katzenjammer kids'>, for <'rheingold beer'>, for <'chucklehead'>.

The Katzenjammer Kids because they were part of his earliest memory, sitting in his father's lap and being read to from the Sunday funnies. Rheingold beer he remembered being in the icebox. And "chucklehead" had been his father's name for him when he was little.

Chucklehead. Why chucklehead? What was its derivation? Why had it died out?

———

They should have saved him. They should have saved the boy from 1926, pried his feet from the painted plaster, brought him with them to Indiana, placed him on the bookcase next to the USRA Mikado.

That and the Boston Braves on TBS, and a model of the USS Shadwell atop the TV. 1:245. A scale world to breathe in. To move in without pain, loss, regret.

About a month after the second attempt the son had made a dogleg from Washington on his way back to San Jose and gone to visit his father. He was back in the Harpswell House by then, able again to get to the dining room for meals, to sit in his power recliner and watch TV. He joked with the staff, teased the kitchen help. They called him "Trouble." "Here comes Trouble," they said, as the eighty-five-year-old man made his slow, misshapen way along the corridor. They knew, of course, but they played along. It almost seemed as if he were happy. Teasing, almost flirting. He was blossoming out, his sister said.

But when the son knocked on his father's door the second morning there had come from inside the room a tremendous groan. A horrible, animal sound. He knew from Jean that getting out of bed was the worst. A flame of pain that ran from his hip to his spine into his head. The son had opened the door and stepped inside in time to see the father standing on the other side of the bed with his face trying to recover. Smiling, for god's sake.

(What his first wife had liked about him—had found sweet, endearing—was the bashful, little-boy-lost, eyes-averted teasing. She had slipped easily into the game, always had a ready comeback for him. He had renamed one of the factories on the railroad after her. Annelise Industries. And he'd urged his son the chucklehead to buy stock in it, a sly compliment to the wife whose pretty face beamed as she teased back, "Don't you sass now!" She was from Georgia. He had left her because she wasn't intellectual enough, didn't read Stephen Jay Gould or Elaine Pagels, didn't know who V. S. Naipaul was.)

"They're sanding me away," his father said that morning after he'd made it around the foot of the bed and into his Assist-a-Lift chair. He held up a piece of pumice stone. "The nurses. They're sanding me away."

———

The Katzenjammer Kids' names were Hans and Fritz. There was Mama and Der Captain and Der Inspector. They spoke in outrageous accents, Mama spanking them with an "Ach, Himmel!," Hans and Fritz gleefully eyeing the snoring Captain—"Mit such snortling only dynamite could vake him!"—and in the next panel attaching an outboard motor to the Captain's bed, sending him putt-putting out to sea.

Who knew? Maybe that was it, the strip that had been read to him, sitting on his father's lap on a Sunday afternoon, in Eisenhower's America.

———

He tried to get his sister to talk to him. Did they not have a responsibility to help their father? He was in pain. He could not deliver himself. Was there not a moral obligation on the adult children to ease the parent's hurt? Had he not done that for them when they were little, picked them up when they had fallen, held them until the pain was gone? They were not a religious family: there was no question of the soul, of trespass on God-given property. His mind was sound. The prospect of unbearable pain was not a prelude to *non compos mentis* but a spur to rational decision. How could they not help him?

She sat in an overstuffed chair, feet pulled up under her, arms crossed as if to lock herself in. She had had breast cancer five years ago and one of her breasts, he knew, was gone.

"I can't," she said.

He went at it again, laid out the ethics of it, the logic. He knew he sounded like a lawyer, but he also believed what he was saying. He asked her if *she* were dying, in horrible pain, with nothing to look forward to but the pain worsening, her personality reduced to drugged-out nothingness, would she not want someone to help her? Would *she* not want him, her brother, to help her kill herself?

"Yes," she said.

Then . . . ?

She looked out the window at the white birches with their leaves gone. "I can't do it."

Okay, then he needed to know if he went it alone, if he talked to their father and found that they were on the same page, if he did it—not this weekend, but soon, before it was too late—if the police came to talk to her afterwards could she tell them she didn't know anything about it? Could she do that? Could he rely on her?

(His second wife hadn't liked any of them—father, mother, daughter, and as it turned out, son. She had said the father had Avoidant Personality Disorder, that he displayed a withdrawn pattern with core features of shyness, dysphoria, distorted cognition in relation to self-effacement. The model railroad was a paradigmatic case of magical thinking. Some people had astrology, alien abduction, Atlantis to make them feel empowered. His father found narcissistic omnipotence in a scale model recreation of Clifton circa 1926. She recommended the triazolobenzodiazepine drug Alprazolam. His father named a casket factory after her.)

———

Chucklehead, according to the *Online Webster's Dictionary*, was "a stupid, gauche person; BLOCKHEAD; DOLT;" and derived from the obsolete adjective *chuckle*, meaning "clumsy" or "stupid," which in turn derived "[perh. irreg. fr.]" the now dialect "chuck," meaning "a log or lump." which in turn gave itself to the term for a cut of dressed beef consisting of the neck and part of the shoulder ("chuck steak," "ground chuck"), which in turn described the lumpish, shouldery shape of a lathe or drill press chuck, his father having been a master machinist.

He clicked on the little speaker icon, let the laptop call him "chucklehead."

———

The next time he flew in, his father was in a wheelchair. He had to be helped out of bed, helped into the wheelchair, wheeled from his room down to the dining hall. He had to be helped on and off the toilet. The nurse disbursed his pain medication in daily rations, standing over him while he took it to make sure he wasn't squirreling it away. There was a noticeable drop in his abilities, in his concentration, in his memory. He had begun to drift, sometimes to repeat himself.

"I waited too long," he said on the second day of the visit. They were sitting on the little deck the Harpswell House had in the rear of the building, watching the chickadees fly to and from a birdfeeder. Though the son had practiced sentences on the airplane, ways of bringing the matter up, he hadn't been able to do it the day before. Now his father was going to do it for him.

"Too long for what?"

The old man made a finger-pistol and raised it to his temple. The son nodded, like of course, he understood.

"There's a way," he said, quietly.

"Too late."

"There's a way with a plastic bag."

The father dropped his eyes, stared at his lap. He'd already tried that, he said after a minute. He had made "a dry run" and had found the suffocation too awful. The plastic stuck to your face.

"Yes," the son intoned gently. One of his legs—how strange!—was quivering inside his pant leg. "But there's a way."

And he detailed the Hemlock Society's method: Seconal to

calm you, plastic bag held on by rubber bands or pantyhose, a painter's mask to keep the plastic from being sucked into the mouth and nostrils, a baseball hat to keep it off your face. He had practiced saying this, ran through it now as if he were back in law school, in moot court where he'd always had his arguments memorized.

"A painter's mask," his father was repeating. His face registered the ingenuity of it. "That might work."

———

On eBay there was a purse with W.W. Mertz on the label. He clicked on the enlargement, studied the name of the department store of his childhood. Just the sight of the familiar letters brought back to him the smell of perfume, the salesladies behind their glass cases with the makeup and lipstick. The mezzanine with its balustrade, the elevator operator in his uniform. How many afternoons had he gone there after school to smell the baseball mitts, to browse through the records? Hi-Fidelity albums for $2.99, Stereophonic $3.99. Standing on the narrow wood flooring and reading through the song titles, trying to decide. They were long gone now, those wooden floors. The salesladies with their costume jewelry. The winter afternoons.

The purse was from the late 1950s, the eBay description said, a black leather bucket purse with peach faille lining, in fine to excellent condition. It didn't mention the stitching.

Was everybody like this? he wondered. Did the past, the inconsequential past, seem to everyone so monstrous? He could have understood it if it were the meaningful past that haunted him—his draft number, say, or the time he'd tried to kiss Elizabeth Skibisky and she'd laughed at him. But this, this awe of the ruined everyday—the way the wallpaper of his childhood bedroom had become so full of consequence, of dread—what did it mean?

———

His father had never once phoned him. Never, not when he was away at college, at law school. Or later when he was married, when his children were born or when they had their birthdays. Not once. He was sure of it.

"Maybe you can't get free," he said now. "That'd be okay."

"No, I can come."

"Okay. All right."

"If you're sure you want me."

There had been a pause on the line, and then a too-emphatic voice, a voice trying not to be frightened: "What the heck, it's time!"

———

There was no Elizabeth Skibisky. No matter what he typed, or how he tried to manipulate the search engine. There were no Skibiskys in Clifton anymore, in the whole of Connecticut. What had happened to her? Married and remarried, name changed, dead? How could he find her?

(All the bourbon from the minibar was gone. It was midnight; the police weren't coming. He'd have to start on scotch.)

———

He had done his research. It was not illegal in the state of Indiana to be present at a suicide. It was only illegal to assist. Just what might constitute assistance would be up to the local DA.

He carried onto the plane, in his attorney's briefcase, a half bottle of Seconal, a painter's mask, a Glad turkey-roasting bag, a Boston Braves baseball cap, an icebag, a pair of his current wife's pantyhose, the Hemlock Society pamphlet, and a pair of rubber gloves. He would have to make sure that the Seconal bottle and the rubber gloves were disposed of afterwards.

He got a room at the Indianapolis Hyatt. He had an idea Jean would not want him staying at the house.

In the rental car he tried for the hundredth time to think what they would say when the time came, what symbolic, ritual thing would ease the terrible moment. But there was nothing.

There had been no center to their lives together, and there was nothing that they could call on now. He doubted if they would even be able to say they loved one another. And yet it was an act of love, wasn't it? what he was doing?

He reached Jean on the cell phone. She had spent the afternoon with their father, had dropped hints about her brother flying in that evening but the old man wouldn't come clean. And no, he had not said goodbye in any special way. She had tried, but he wouldn't let her.

When he drove up to the Harpswell House his father was sitting crumpled in his wheelchair, facing the front door, waiting. He had a magazine on his lap. When his son came through the door he held up the front cover.

"Makes me nostalgic," he said.

It was an illustrator's painting of a New England homestead in winter: white clapboard siding and black shutters, split-rail fence, cozy pasture and waiting sleigh. There was smoke curling from the chimney.

"For what?" the son found himself asking. His father turned the magazine back to himself, blinked, screwed up his mouth.

"I don't know," he said and laughed as though the joke was on him. He tossed the magazine onto a nearby chair.

"You're all going to vanish," he told an aide as they went slowly down the corridor. He made a magic-wand arabesque in the air. "Little Willy the Magician!"

"Little Willy the Troublemaker, you mean!" the aide called with her nursing-home bonhomie. She smiled after them, watched them go.

Under his voice his father muttered, "Yeah, yeah, yeah."

Down in his room he had divided his possessions into two piles, one on either side of the table. There were photographs of the Clifton house, of Jean's wedding, of Annelise. There was a photo of their mother circa 1943 with a come-hither look that the son had never seen before. There was his honorable discharge from the service. A micrometer. Scale model plans for the roundhouse at the Waterbury yard. In front of each pile was a kind of place card. "Jean" one of them said; the other said "William."

"Self-evident," his father said with a wave of his hand.

———

He remembered—strange! where did such a memory come from?—he couldn't have been but five or six: they were walking, the four of them, along an abandoned railroad right-of-way. It was the sort of thing they did Sunday afternoons: his father with paper and pencil, tape measure in hand, his sister collecting leaves, and he, little William, holding his mother's hand and negotiating the weeds between the railroad ties. His father would go ahead of them, writing things down, "checking for ghosts," he said, finding the occasional foundation of a way house or a shed, and taking measurements. From time to time he would stand up and look around at the blue-green trees, listen to the buzzing meadow, as if he could somehow see, somehow hear, in a world which was presently in ruins, a past that was alive and lit with meaning.

But on that day, on the day he remembered now with such peculiar clarity, his father had gotten too far ahead of them and the son, watching him grow smaller, losing him from time to time behind a bush or a leafy branch, had gotten scared and begun to cry. His mother had picked him up and carried him, told him it was all right, pointed at his father ahead of them— see?—and yet still he had cried, full of childish dread, stretching his arms out to his father who had stopped just where the roadbed curved into the dark trees, his pant legs in bright sun, his head and shoulders in shadow, turned for a moment to look back at them, smiling, waving to them . . .

———

They did a dry run. He helped his father out of the wheelchair and into bed, laid out the items from his briefcase. They tried the painting mask first, just to get used to breathing through it. Then he helped put the baseball cap on, then after a minute the icebag. That was so he would keep cool, the son explained. It would get hot once the plastic bag was on. Was he all right? Was it comfortable? The son did everything with the plastic gloves on. He didn't want his fingerprints on anything.

They tried the plastic bag. He waited a few minutes and then mock-tied the panty hose on, showed the father how he was to slip his fingers between the hose and his neck whenever he wanted to breathe. The Seconal would eventually put him to sleep, but until then he could breathe whenever he wanted. Did he understand? Was he okay?

They took the items off, one by one.

It was then that his father told him about the Shadwell, about the torpedo, about standing around on deck waiting to sink, having to relieve himself.

"It's hard to kill little Willy, you know," he said. He went through a funny pantomime his son hadn't seen since childhood: licking a make-believe stamp on the tip of his thumb, then stamping it on his chest like a badge of approval. "Twice now," he said, "three times if you include the Japs." He made his little chuckle; then: "How long's it take those pills to work?"

The son said twenty minutes, maybe half an hour.

He nodded, looked off into space, then over at his nightstand. He twiddled his thumbs, laughed. "Ever show you this?" he asked and lifted a toy off the nightstand that the doctors had given him. It was a battery-powered gizmo—Pull it! Bop it! Twist it!—about the size and shape of a nightstick. The son had seen it before. When you turned it on it commanded you to pull a lever or bop a button or twist a shaft. If you did it quickly enough the thing whistled with glee, if you didn't it screamed bloody murder at you. It was supposed to help maintain coordination and reflex.

Now when the old man turned it on and the thing cried "Bop it!" he pulled instead and got screamed at. He let the toy fall to the floor.

"Story of my life," he said. He shrugged, whistled a little tune, then: "Well, let's have them."

The son kept himself from saying anything. It was one of the rules he'd set: if it turned out his father had worked up the courage, then he would not get in the way. And yet as he handed the pills two by two to the old man, helped him drink, he knew he had been half-hoping his father would call it off. He was a timid man, wasn't he? The world had been too much for him, hadn't it? But it was the son who found himself having to suppress the stirrings of panic.

"Now what? We wait?"

It was a horrible place to die. He didn't mean the Harpswell House—which was horrible in its own way—but Belmont, Indiana, so far from the New England of their birth, even if the New England of their birth was not the New England of magazine covers but a nineteenth-century mill town gone to twentieth-century ruin. Why didn't his father mind? This exile from everything that he knew—the flat land, the cornfields, the southern-inflected accents of the people. It was, once again, as if the outside world didn't matter, as if what mattered was what he carried within—his model railroad like a gene in the recesses of his personality, carried into the Opportunity Room when he was five years old, into the engine room of the USS Shadwell, into the deep sleep of a dozen Seconal.

"I feel funny."

The son looked up in time to see his father's eyes flutter closed, then open. "It's the drug," he said.

The old man looked around, looked at the wheelchair, at the mirror, at the door. It was as if he were checking on the world.

"The bag?" he asked.

"When you start to get sleepy."

He nodded. He had his hands folded on his lap.

There had to be something else, the son thought. There had to be more. He had half an impulse to apologize, to say he was sorry for something, maybe sorry for not loving Annelise as he should have. And then he thought he should get up, go get the 2-8-2, give it to his father, let him hold it. But it seemed stupid, corny, a *gesture*. His hands were hot inside the rubber gloves.

On the other side of the wall someone flushed a toilet. His father's breathing grew regular, deep.

"Dad?" he said when a few more minutes had passed. The old man stirred.

"What?"

The plastic bag lay at the foot of the bed. He did not want to make the decision himself if his father fell asleep.

"Is it time?"

The son couldn't help himself: "You don't have to do it," he said. The old man managed to open his eyes. He blinked, tried to rouse himself. He motioned for the gear.

"Now or never."

"You can just sleep."

Again, the gesture. Tired, over and done with. "C'mon."

He watched his hands do it—the painter's mask, the baseball cap, the plastic bag, the pantyhose. And then he heard himself show his father again how to let air into the bag when he needed it. The old man nodded, seemed to smile behind the painter's mask: he understood. After a minute the plastic bag began to cloud with condensation.

What he remembered then—idly, inconsequentially—was how his father had used to like putting his eye down to track level, watching the trains from the vantage of a scale-model person. They looked real that way, he'd said. What the son had liked was the vista leading into Clifton, the granite bluffs and the Naugatuck River below, the track snaking its way alongside the acrylic water—it *had* looked real, hadn't it?—the scrubby junipers clinging to the cliffs, a heron wading in a sheltered pool. He had used to sit on the cellar stairs and watch his father work, forbidden to help but sitting there anyway and imagining—

"It's not my fault," his father said suddenly from under the painter's mask. The son's eyes snapped back. He could barely see inside the bag for the condensation.

"What?" he managed to say.

"It's all been forced on me," the father murmured and he lifted his arm in a gesture that somehow included the room around him, the middle-aged figure of his son, and the dull sound of the world outside the window. It was the last thing he said.

———

He had turned the computer off. He had turned the lights off. He stood at the hotel window looking out at the twenty-first-century city, at the pyramids of light and the postmodern office towers. He had his cellphone in hand. He had just woken his wife up.

"It's over," was the first thing he said. He could hear her stirring, sitting up in bed.

"William?"

"We did it. It's done."

"Good lord," she said. "Are you all right?"

He was all right. He wanted to tell her all about it, if she could bear hearing about it. Not now, he said, but when he got home. And he would tell her about all these things he'd been looking up on the web. And about this day he kept remembering, this day when he was little and they were all out walking along an abandoned railroad track and he had gotten scared. But even as he said it—even as he listened for sounds of sympathy in her voice, for a sign that things were all right, that she wanted him back home—he felt how impossible it was, how far away he was, and how he would never be able to tell her, never get her to see that summer day . . . the dark greenery that had seemed so threatening to his five-year-old mind, the curving withdrawal of the roadbed, the eerie buzz of a cicada, the invisible life that seemed to palpate in the tall grass, in the eddying trees, the aquamarine, the sunny gold, the way his father had smiled back at them, back at his crying son in his wife's arms, the way he had waved to them—and then turned and stepped into the dark-green shade.

Moral Problem #2:
THE BALLAD OF LITTLE HOMO

Okay, this is the scene: You're wearing your murder-ones and the world's got that dark, smoked look you love. You're hanging with your *vatos* at the corner of Euclid and Whittier and there's a serious philosophical discussion underway. You've got to strike the right pose when serious philosophical discussions are underway, so in addition to the dark glasses you've got your sea-green drape wide at the shoulders tight at the rear, your raspberry-colored shirt to add just the right touch, and on your feet your new Stacy Adams. If anybody messes with the knife-edge crease in your pants there's the .44 Bulldog strapped against your ribs. That about covers it.

Over at the curb Psycho Chico is mad-dogging every car that pulls up at the stoplight. He is not paying attention to the philosophical discussion.

It's Plato doing most of the talking. College fucked up Plato something bad and you can hardly understand what he says anymore. But all the *vatos* listen because he's Plato, you know? What he's on about now is moving the gang out of banging into something more intellectually satisfying. That's what he says, "intellectually satisfying." From behind your murder-ones you catch Extra Cheese's eye and the look that passes between you is messed up for sure. But you don't want to disrespect Plato so you think you'll just check out for a minute or two, let the smoke take over, observe the world at the corner of Euclid and

Whittier: the Saturday-night lowriders on parade, the *chicas* going by with their asses in the air, the pizza smell, the taillights smearing the boulevard, and the six of you—Plato, Psycho Chico, Extra Cheese, Inca, Little Inca, and you, Homo—hanging in your *trapos* like a *Vanity Fair* photographer is due any minute.

"¡Qué es el vigio!" Psycho Chico shouts at a carful of Americans. He shows them his gun from out of his waistband and they take off, right through the red light. You laugh, everybody laughs. The smoke gets handed to you from Little Inca's direction.

It's got something to do with gambling, what Plato's on about, only he doesn't mean *that* gambling, it's *metaphysical* gambling he means. (Man, it hurts your brain listening to this *vato*.) Like you are all the victims of fate, chance, shit like that.

"Like hanging here," Plato says, "inviting a bullet."

Extra Cheese and you exchange looks: you are hanging here *offering* bullets is what you and Extra Cheese are doing, Psycho Chico too, though you might be willing to admit Plato's is another way of looking at it. Streetcorner roulette, he calls it. He likes saying this so much, he says it again, then hangs back, looks you all over. He's got his pants pegged and that cool white *tando* but you are beginning to wonder about him. *Probability*, he says like he's taking out his double deuce, only it's words instead of bullets.

"Man, what you on?"

"Like last Christmas, when Little Homo got jumped in that fucked-up jack." He purposely doesn't look at you. Little Homo was your brother. This is some sore shit for you and your heart.

"Check out the variables," Plato says. "Suppose that night we hang on the northbound instead of the southbound. Or we don't go after the Honda, but wait for something with more *huevos*. The variables, man—"

But you are remembering that night. The sorry-ass Christmas decorations on the avenue. The cold that made you want to jack in the first place. You were wearing your Killer 54's and your Ben Davis pants. Little Homo was khakied down, except with sandals so his feet were cold. When the Honda pulled up it was you who went and stood in front of the bumper so they couldn't scoot, Inca at the rear, and Little Homo flashing his 9 millimeter at the driver's window. There was the terror-struck face you could see through the windshield, and Little Inca laughing, and then the car you should've seen drawing alongside the Honda, the cherried-out Galaxie you should've recognized before the window rolled down, before the single-shot stuck out its sawed-off nose, before Little Homo was blown against the side of the Honda, the back of his shirt suddenly crimson, and before he collapsed on the pavement, looking up at you and whispering your name, not Homo, but your *name*, man: Luis! Luis!

"You're all fucked," Plato is saying. "What you got to do is be fucked on your own terms."

"¿Y qué?" Psycho Chico says. He's come over from the curbside.

"You got to take control, man," Plato says and he draws himself up, throws his shoulders back, like there, he's said it.

"What, exactly, do we got to take control *of*?" you say.

He still doesn't look at you. He's got his eyes swinging out over the boulevard like there's something to see. "You got to eliminate the middleman," he says.

And then—it is one of the coolest things you will ever see—he does it. He takes from out of its strap his Redhawk with the blued barrel, flicks open the cylinder and lets the cartridges fall out of their chambers into his hand. Then he takes one of them between his fingers, shows it around the circle like a magician making sure everyone sees he's legit, and then slips it into the revolver. He closes the cylinder and gives it a spin. You want to say something, you want to put out your hand, touch his arm, but it's too beautiful to stop, too cool, too righteous. He lifts the revolver to his temple. He smiles, finally looks at you, at each of the *vatos*, and then the hammer is drawing back, in slow-motion like a Jackie Chan movie. . . . And then there is the click, the empty click.

"Shit, man," says Inca, who never says anything.

"*Ese*," Extra Cheese murmurs.

But you are rooted to the sidewalk. Even when Psycho Chico spits and takes the revolver from Plato, gives the cylinder a spin and with a fuck-you look puts it to his own temple, even then you can't move, can't move even when there's an explosion somewhere and a piece of Psycho Chico's skull spins into your white chinos leaving a map of blood you will never wash out—because you know a new world has happened, you have been given a new world and the question is, *ese*, what are you going to do with it?

BEING AND NOTHINGNESS
(NOT A REAL TITLE)

In the next room Incunabula de la Luz (not her real name) is auditioning people to be her mother. Her real mother—at least she *claims* to be her real mother—wanted to come to the auditions, but Luz—Lucita—said no. So this is how come I'm on the phone doing the play-by-play.

"Overcoats," I'm saying. "Most of them have got these drab, 1940s-ish overcoats on."

"Wool or synthetic?" Lucita's mother asks.

"Wool," I say, "definitely wool."

"Jewish?"

I consider. "Maybe Jewish. Probably some Jewish."

Is that a clue? Am I living with a Jessica, a Rachel? Is it a Miriam I'm in love with?

"And the Serpent's Tooth," Lucita's mother says, "what's she saying? What's she asking them?"

The Serpent's Tooth. This is a new piece of information.

"I believe she's asking them about her first period."

"Oh, God! Oh, mother of Jesus!"

So maybe not Jessica. Maybe Maria, Teresa, Consuelo.

"And do they know? Are they saying what happened?"

Of course they aren't. They can't know, can they? They're *improvising,* aren't they?

"Yes," I answer. "I believe they are."

"They *can't* be! They're actors!"

"It's a mystery," I agree.

There's about seven of them. Mothers, I mean. They've taken over the living room—*my* living room; I pay the rent—and I'm out in the hall standing in my stocking feet with the cordless. Through the half-open door I can just hear Lucita's shy, quiet, downcast, sexy, drive-me-crazy voice. Tomorrow it's her boyfriend she's holding auditions for. Ha-ha. Like, get it?

"*Oy!*" Lucita's mother says in my ear. "*Mamma mia!*" she says.

But I've got my plans. I've got my ways and devices. And one of my ways is this: when we make love and Lucita's on the point of coming I call her Diane—*oh, Diane!* I say. Or Dolores—*oh, Dolores!* I say. Next up is Elizabeth, Erica, Erin. Then Fanny, Franny, Geraldine, Gertrude, Grace: alphabetical, in case you didn't notice. I keep a book on my nightstand, one of those choose-your-baby's-name books. I figure I'll hit with one of them. One of them will interrupt her train of thought, break her concentration. But it hasn't happened so far. At least I haven't seen any sign. But she's sly, Lucita is. Capable of duplicity, misdirection. And even though I'm an edgy kind of guy myself—I mean I've got my own edge, even if I was a mechanical engineering major—still, with Lucita I'm aware I may be out of my league.

In the meantime there's a lot of names between now and Zelda. It could be worse.

———

The first time I saw her I was cutting across Copley Square on my way to lunch with my friend Siegfried. She was seated at this table in the middle of the square with a white tablecloth across it, dressed like a nurse. There was an easel beside her, one of those boardroom presentation sort of easels, and a poster on it that said FREE CASTS. But Siegfried was on about his many suspicions and I'm his good friend and a good friend's job is to listen, right? So I didn't give the nurse a second look.

But an hour later on my way back to work I'm alone, so now I give her a second look. This nurse's outfit she's got on, it's some sort of World War I English job—you know, the starched white dress, the darling little cape about the shoulders, every button done up, hat pinned to hair. Cute. Sexy, if you go in for that sort of thing and who doesn't? She's just sitting there. She's got surgical scissors and plaster of paris and a tub of water. Free casts. But there're no takers. No one's even giving her a hard time though the square is littered with the usual derelicts. Taped to the front of her table there's this Red Cross sign, but you can see it's just construction paper.

"So, like, what's this?" I say.

"Free casts, sir," she says in this spot-on British accent.

So I'm thinking, okay, this is like performance art or something. I look around for a camera. Then I cross the space between us, right up to her table, and I smile at her because my smile is the only thing about me you might be inclined to call handsome.

"Would you like a free cast, sir?"

Really, the accent's a killer. And she's looking straight up at me but you can tell it's an act. You can tell she's shy, that ordinarily she's got the sidelong thing going, but that right now she's being an English nurse in the Great War, which requires the brave front, direct if polite address, etc.

There's a business card on her table, so I pick it up, read it. You know what it says? It says *Incunabula de la Luz (not her real name)*. For real. I mean *not her real name* is right there on the business card. And then there's her phone number with, you guessed it, *not her real phone number* after it.

"Incunabula," I say.

"Yes, sir?"

"I'm a vocabulary freak, Incunabula," I say, mock-scolding her with my forefinger, "so I know what this means."

"Gracious, sir!"

She doesn't look at all English. Her skin isn't pale or peachy, and her hair is dark. She looks more Mediterranean. Maybe in the Sephardic direction. To tell you the truth she looks like an Incunabula is what she looks like. Which, in case you're not a vocabulary freak is a term used to designate books published in the first half-century after the invention of the printing press. State Capitals for four hundred, Alex.

"Which arm is it, sir?"

So I sit down in the chair alongside the table and, because I'm a lefty, give her my right arm. She unbuttons the shirt cuff, rolls up the sleeve, and starts touching me. She probes my forearm, gently, professionally, looking for the break. I have to say it feels good. Her hands know how to touch, if you know what I mean.

"How did you hurt yourself, sir?"

I don't answer, watch instead as she readies the plaster-soaked squares. She does it with skill and care. Or the simulacrum of skill and care.

"Did you take a tumble?"

I'm trying to catch her eye. But she's intent upon her work, bent over my arm so all I can see is the top of her head. And her temple where there're these little wisps of hair that aren't obeying the hairstyle. And her eyebrows drizzling off into nowhere. These are the sort of details of face and figure which, were one going to fall in love with Incunabula de la Luz, one would find inexplicably charming.

"My arm's not actually broken," I say to see if I can maybe throw her off her game. "I don't need a cast."

"Everybody needs a cast," she says.

"I don't."

"Sir?" she says and lifts her eyes to me in inquiry. "No injuries? No hurts?"

So okay, now I get it. She wants to move us into the hall of mirrors. Metaphor, metonymy, malleable signifiers. But I don't bite. No way am I going to be drawn out on how Megan/Beth/Denise serially broke my heart. Not part of the situation here.

"Nice try," I say.

But she doesn't pick up the challenge, goes back to work instead, and I don't press the advantage. If that's what it is.

"Don't be alarmed if it begins to feel warm," she says when she's done. "That will just be the plaster curing." She busies herself cleaning up, washes her hands. "You will need to keep the cast on for two weeks."

"Two weeks," I repeat.

"May I have your address?" she asks, pen poised over the flip side of one of her business cards. I consider the request a moment, then tell her my address. I throw in my name as a freebie. Which is William, by the way. Bill.

"Only two weeks?" I say.

She regards me from under those brows. "Two weeks will be sufficient, sir. It will begin the healing." Then she's looking past me, all nurse-efficient, ignoring the palpable metaphor. She calls "Next!" with perfect aplomb. Though there's no next waiting in line.

So for two weeks I wear the cast. I'm a gamer. I can appreciate the absurd, the amphigoric. I figure it's fifty-fifty I'm never going to see her again—it's a joke, a bit of Dadaist clowning, right? But like I say, I've got an appreciation for the absurd even if I was a mechanical engineering major, and completion, carrying through on my part has its rewards even if I'm the only one watching. And besides, I figure if I'm going to have any chance at being the recipient of any, you know, *favors*, the cast has definitely got to be on my arm if and when she actually shows up at my apartment. We understand one another on this point, yes?

One of the first things I do of course is I call the number on her business card but it really isn't her number. Which is disheartening because I somehow had the idea that putting down a fake number, plus calling it a fake number, would somehow make it a real number, like multiplying minuses. So then I Google her—which is what we do with the mysteries nowadays, don't we?—and bango! there she is, thousands of hits. Turns out Incunabula de la Luz is famous in an edgy, underground sort of way. Famous first of all for being a founding member of the Surveillance Camera Players, which was this troupe that went around Boston in the late nineties performing in front of surveillance cameras. I mean like doing *Hamlet* and episodes of the *Mary Tyler Moore Show* in parking garages and ATM cubicles, with no audience except some low-fidelity videotape machine, doomed to be watched by exactly nobody unless a crime got itself simultaneously committed. Another thing she did was erect these crucified bunny rabbits on Easter. She and her gang took these pink stuffed bunnies with their cute smiley bunny noses and nailed them to crosses, stuck a crown of thorns on their heads, etc., and put them all over the city. This rang a bell because I recalled there having been one on the steps leading up to the Metropolitan District Commission on Somerset Street which is where I work. It was pretty funny, I guess.

There was more, but you get the picture. Basically, she's an artist.

"Dude, that's like Cacophony Society stuff," says my friend Siegfried when I explain to him about my cast and Incunabula de la Luz and the stuff on the web. We're riding the elevators in the Sheraton. We're not inside the elevators, understand, we're on *top* of them, the shaft rising twelve stories above our heads, the massive counterweights plummeting on either side of us. It's a thing we do from back when we were undergrads. The Massachusetts Institute of Technology Elevator Surfers.

"It's art," I say. "It's not cacophony."

"Totally cacophony," he says. He has this adversarial thing with The Cacophony Society, which is a real society of real misfits devoted to committing pointless acts of senselessness. He was a mechanical engineering major too.

"She means something by it," I say, though truthfully I can't be sure. She may not mean anything at all and it's just me *reading* meaning into it, into the feel of her fingers, into the Surveillance Camera Players and the crucified bunnies.

"Incidental," says Siegfried. "The meaning is just part of the noise. Depend upon it, Watson, she's an aspiring cacophonist. You better let me help you take the cast off."

We're stopped somewhere in the mid-floors. People are getting on, getting off. They don't know we're here, two griffins, two gargoyles above them. My last name, by the way, is Watson. For ten years now this has supplied Siegfried with no end of recreation.

Of course, with some of the surveillance cameras, you've got to figure there is an audience—some sad, flatulent, hemorrhoidal security guard in a windowless room with a dozen black-and-white monitors suddenly seeing instead of a blurry nothing a blurry Lou Grant with a blurry Mary Richards about to deliver herself of a piece of her mind. This probably doesn't make a difference.

"I'm getting used to it," I tell Siegfried, turning the cast over this way, that way. Truth is, the itching is driving me crazy. When I'm alone I take this plastic serrated knife I've got and I poke it up under the cast and have at it.

"Okay," Siegfried sighs. He pats me on the knee, looks upward into ten stories of grease and gloom. "Just don't go over to the other side, Watson. I need you."

Which, in case you didn't know it, was the first thing anybody ever said over a telephone. Alexander Graham Bell in one room spilling battery acid and saying that to his assistant in another room. Watson, I need you. This probably doesn't make a difference either.

———

When the day comes—the two-week day—I call in sick and hang out at home. I've got the apartment picked up, though not too picked up, and I've put on this black shirt, though not too black. *Being and Nothingness* is out on the kitchen table—I mean

I'm actually reading it—but I figure that that's a bit over the top, so I slip the book into the microwave and lay out instead my copy of The House of Mirth, floppy and paraplegic from when Denise broke all the spines on all my books (a note would have sufficed, Denise). My cast has been signed by my co-workers. It makes it look like I've got friends.

I imagine the knock at the door so often that morning— brisk, no-nonsense—that when I actually hear a brisk, no-nonsense knock I don't get up at first, just sit there reading The House of Mirth like what? This is one of the problems of living alone. There are others.

"Keeping our spirits up, sir?" is the first thing she says when she's in my living room, turning around to face me. She's in her nurse outfit still. There was a moment there—rewind the tape—when she couldn't quite hide her pleasure at seeing the cast still on my arm.

We decide the kitchen table is the place for the job at hand. I note her note The House of Mirth (female author, female main character, artistic soul unappreciated by superficial society: good choice, Watson). Out of this little black bag she takes a pair of surgical scissors, then these other scissors that look like they mean business and she starts in, professional, practiced, intent upon her work, head bowed so that there they are again, the wisps of hair that won't get with the program.

When the cast is off she washes my arm and dear God it's nice to feel someone touch you, isn't it?

"There," she says when she's patted my arm dry. "All better," she says.

And then she's putting her things away, standing up. It's now or never, Watson. But I can't think of anything to say.

What saves me is the phone suddenly ringing. I excuse myself with a just-a-sec finger in the air. What's the word, Siegfried asks and I tell him the word is consummatum est, trusting he will not be misled by the phrase's vista of fruition.

"She's there?" he says.

"Right."

There's a silence on the line, like Siegfried is trying to factor this piece of meaningfulness, meaningfulness not being what he had expected.

"Dude!" he whispers, and that about says it all.

"It's a lovely apartment," Incunabula de la Luz says when I'm off the phone. She's strolling about, doctor's bag held primly in front of her. It's not a lovely apartment, but it's in the coveted North End, the old Italian neighborhood where there aren't any Italians anymore but everyone pretends there is. The apartment costs more than I can afford now that Megan/Beth/Denise is not paying her half.

"I'm thinking of renting a room out," I say though I am not, in fact, thinking of renting a room out.

"Oh?" she says. She gazes around the living room with new significance. "I have a friend who's looking for a place."

So that sounds like a cue, doesn't it? It's our next performance piece, me showing her around the apartment like a landlord, turning the hot water on, turning the hot water off, flushing the toilet, opening cupboards, showing the second bedroom. She grades gradually out of her English accent into an American. It's quite a feat really. I keep up my end pretty well. She asks how much? Are kitchen privileges included? Inspired, I say: "Television off at eleven o'clock." We open and shut the hall closet, turn on the ceiling fan.

"What's your friend's name?" I ask.

"Incunabula," she answers.

"Common name, is it?" I say, without missing a beat. We're back in the kitchen now. She's opening cabinets. Opens the microwave and finds *Being and Nothingness*.

"I'll take it," she says, tucking Sartre under her arm.

Later that afternoon when a taxi brings her back—trunk, suitcase, vase with a single lily—she's dressed like a fourteen-year-old Chicana hottie. She's got the accent to go with it. And the strawberry-flavored hot pants.

———

When the mothers leave they go single-file, yakking, still in their mother mode. They pretty much ignore me standing in the hall. Lucita follows them out, stands in the doorway, waves and calls "Bye, Mom!" "Bye, dear!" a chorus of voices calls back. Then she turns around, smiles at me her lovely, wet, crooked smile, and disappears into her room.

"And tomorrow it's boyfriend auditions?" Siegfried says, an hour later. We're atop elevator number one in Building 18 at MIT. I needed an elevator hit, so here we are.

"Right."

"Not good," he says.

No, it's not. Because unlike a mother, who you'll agree has a certain biological tenacity, a boyfriend is modular. You can unplug one and plug in another. Happens all the time.

"And this is all leading where?" Siegfried asks. "The point of this is what?"

Or put another way: Are the auditions authentic auditions, which is to say, are they auditions for some future performance, or are the auditions themselves the performance, leading to nothing beyond making a stage of my living room, actors of the mothers, and me out in the hallway the only spectator?

Sometimes I have the idea that I should ride in on her like Lochinvar disrupting the wedding banquet, Lochinvar throwing his love across the pommel of his saddle and galloping out of the hall into the melting distance. In our wake there are gasps, expressions of wonder and admiration, and then the realization that beautiful Incunabula de la Luz has been saved from a marriage to Simulation and Charade. Focus, please.

Beside us, elevator number two goes up, goes down.

The Chicana hottie didn't last long. Neither did the Russian countess. What's lasted the longest—five weeks now—is this:

I come home from work and Incunabula de la Luz is there, the *Boston Globe* is there, a martini with a pearl onion is there (I don't care for martinis but there you have it: they're part of the picture, part of the Eisenhower iconic). We talk about our day. My job. We have a son variously named Richie or Mikey or Duke who is always off at Little League or band practice. After dinner we curl up on the couch and watch TV. Incunabula de la Luz (not her real name, alas!) slips her shoes off, pulls her pedal-pushers up under her and nestles her body into mine. It fits. Damn her and her body, but she fits into me like nesting spoons, like the breast of Brazil tucked under the Horn of Africa. I do not dare kiss her at these moments. I do not dare touch her with my hands. It is enough to smell her perfume, to feel the warmth of her body through her clothes. After Leno does his monologue she goes off to her bedroom. I go off to mine.

So okay, you know that whole business about me calling her *Diane* and *Dolores* and *Franny* when we're making love? You remember that? Well, I made that up. I mean I *would* call her all those names if we were actually making love. But that's the part I made up. We're not sleeping together. We don't even kiss. We *almost* kiss. We *almost* make love. But we don't *actually*.

So sue me.

"It's the coefficient of fascination," Siegfried says. He's over on elevator number two now. It's one of the things we do, surfing from one elevator to the other—though only in the older buildings, in the buildings with Otis Glide-Rides and HydroLifts, not in the skyscrapers where the Elevonics are going at warp speed. As of right now, Siegfried is going up and I'm going down. But Building 18 is only eight stories (two underground) so it's not long before he's going down and I'm going up.

"So like, what're you going to do?" he asks when we have our couple of seconds of interface. Then his curly head disappears below.

"I don't know," I say a minute later. I've got more to say so I surf over to elevator number two. Which is seriously dangerous, by the way. And should only be attempted by graduates of MIT. "Question is," I say, "to what degree do we insist upon reality being real?"

He considers this a moment. The elevator stops and someone gets on, says *Damn him!* in a bitter, strangled voice that makes us shut up for three floors. When whoever it is is gone, Siegfried says: "Will insisting get you, you know—how can I put this?—will it get you connubial bliss? I mean, *real* connubial bliss, not *aspiring* connubial bliss?"

"It might," I say, pursing my lips. "And it might not."

He shakes his head so the curls rattle about his face. "Watson," he says, "you have *seen* the facts, but you have not *apprehended* them. This chick is quantum to the core. She is simultaneously absent and present. Her name arrives before she does. If I were you, I'd change the locks."

"Can't," I say.

"Why not?"

"I love her."

He gives his whole body a shake, like a dog ridding itself of water, and jumps back over to elevator number one.

———

When the boyfriends start arriving I hide in my bedroom. Against my better judgment I've decided to give in to the masochism of the moment. I've called in sick again, got some takeout from Mamma Traviata's, and I've got a glass tumbler from the kitchen because I remember from a *Waves* problem-set freshman year that if you want to eavesdrop on someone in the next room what you do is you press a drinking glass against the wall and put your ear to it. Try it. It works.

Here's a question: Who is Incunabula de la Luz when no one is watching? Not like with the Surveillance Camera Players where there's still watching taking place, if only metaphysical watching, but when *really* no one is watching. Like when she's alone in the apartment and I'm off at work. Who is she then? How does she dress? What does her voice sound like? Who is it who I think I love?

Out in the hall I put the drinking glass to the closed door and listen while one of the boyfriends gargles his love for Incunabula de la Luz (not her real name, buster!).

When I'm alone I can tell you who I am. I'm the guy who goes into Incunabula de la Luz's bedroom and paws through her clothes, that's who I am. The English nurse and the Chicana hottie. The Eisenhower Missus. They're all there, identities neatly folded in her bureau, hanging in her closet. Iconic women you can't help but fall in love with. I take out and hold to my heart her culottes and pedal-pushers. Her padded bras and peppermint underpants. I construct serial Incunabulas on the bedspread—tops, bottoms, tights—and yes, I'll admit there's a whiff of sexual arousal in the activity but not, *not*, out of proportion to the stimulus and not, *not*, anything like the arousal caused by the real Incunabula de la Luz, which is healthy and normal. Thank you.

On the hall table there's a printed invitation to the *2nd Annual Lee Harvey Oswald Memorial Shoot*, but Lucita will not be attending. The first *Lee Harvey Oswald Memorial Shoot* was one of her performance pieces, and she disavows this 2nd Annual business as derivative, manqué, artistically inauthentic. Or so she phrased it the day the invitation arrived, carelessly handing me the prim white card like maybe I was derivative too, or would be, Watson, *were you ever to attempt to move your marriage from the Being of make-believe to the Nothingness of the real.*

Back in my bedroom I lay down on my bed, and instead of eating the rigatoni from Mamma Traviata's, I start on a bottle of bourbon. Truth is, I've already had a few hits, can you tell?

And I have to say I do not see how I am being a proper specta-tor. There is nothing to spectate. There is only the sore inside me, the gimpy, inarticulate, inept, abscessed longing to roll around in my mouth like a broken tooth. And the wonder and guessing: Who is she choosing, what actor skilled in duplicity and posturing? What false but functioning surface will emerge as Incunabula de la Luz's boyfriend, and how can Watson with his subcutaneous self ever hope to compete?

By the time the audition breaks up, I am completely sozzled. And it would appear that I have spent the last half-hour string-ing up Lucita's clothes in the hallway. I have evidently used floor lamps for mannequins. The boyfriends look at the array of female selves and then at me like who's the capital-L loser? They have to move one of the floor lamps—in miniskirt and thigh-high boots—in order to exit the apartment. Back in the living room doorway, Lucita is the only one who understands. And she does not like it.

The first time I rode the elevators in the Hancock tower was the day Megan broke up with me. They are the fastest elevators in Boston. Frightening. Unsafe to stand up on. Siegfried won't do them, neither will any of the other surfers we know. But the day Megan left me I went and rode them in a fit of self-destruc-tion, flat on my back, bawling like a lunatic.

But with Incunabula de la Luz and the coefficient of fascina-tion, it's a different story. I am not here to frighten myself out of love. I am here to feel the darkness and the fifty-story shaft disappearing into void, and the reek of grease, and the coun-terweights plunging past in their carriageways. I have come to pit the dependability of physics against the motivating phan-toms. Because the one needs the other, does it not? Does not the one need the other, Incunabula de la Luz?

Back at the apartment, on the hall table where we keep the

telephone, a piece of paper has materialized with a list of names and numbers—Lucita's new family. At the bottom is a date, a time, an address. It is like a handkerchief, deftly dropped.

Incunabula de la Luz—you with your slim hips moving like phantoms inside your inconstant clothes—what is it you want from your audience?

———

When the day of the performance arrives I lurk in the apartment while she readies herself in her room—her clothes, her persona, the being and nothingness of it all. When finally she calls good-bye and I hear the apartment door close behind her, I get my own things together and follow her. No Sherlockian disguise, just Watson in all his Watsonness. I don't even bother to keep much of a distance between us as we walk; on the Red Line platform stand a mere fifty feet from her as we wait for the T. She's dressed in the iconic grunge of our teenage years: too-big T-shirt, underwear visible through the frayed seat of her jeans. She doesn't acknowledge my presence. The train rumbles into the station like a curtain going up.

Ten minutes later we're walking through South Boston, past working-class triple-deckers and dented Toyotas. When she turns in at a rundown duplex, I continue a little ways down the sidewalk, and then stop and turn back. The house is gray and sad, with dingy shutters, and a swaybacked porch where a teenaged Lucita might or might not have sat summer nights with her girlfriends. She goes up the stairs and unlocks the door, calls "Mom?" for the benefit of the audience out on the sidewalk, and leaves the door ajar behind her.

I spend the next fifteen minutes leaning against a parked car out front as the members of Lucita's family arrive one by one and go inside the house. When the Boyfriend arrives—tall, smooth-faced—I think I have seen him before in some hardware store commercial.

"Going to the audition?" I say, advancing on him from

behind. We are, of course, beyond the point of auditioning. We are the Boyfriend and the boyfriend, and we enter the house together, one of us with his television handsomeness, the other clutching the cacophony of his love like a life preserver. We go down a stairway into a basement playroom with the forlorn look of all such places. Water-stained carpet, abandoned toys. A circle of chairs has been set up. There is the Mother, the Father, the Favorite Aunt, the Best Friend from down the street, and now the Boyfriend. The other boyfriend sits in a chair perhaps reserved for the Audience, perhaps not. On the walls are stick-on planets, all except Venus which has fallen down, perhaps years ago. In the center of the circle the performance artist Incunabula de la Luz raises her hands like a conductor.

And not for the first time, it occurs to me that Siegfried may be right, that among other things it is Lucita herself who is behind the 2nd Annual Lee Harvey Oswald Memorial Shoot. That she has sent the invitation to herself, staged the derivative as an extension of the original, and that her subsequent disdain—standing in my hallway sifting through the day's mail with me as audience—was only a subterfuge to lure me further onstage.

Beside me the Boyfriend's skin is lacquered with the color of television. We sit and wait for the performance to begin.

Somebody, I have decided, has to stick up for reality.

When the time comes for the Boyfriend to speak of his love for Incunabula de la Luz, I will counter by speaking of my love for Incunabula de la Luz; when he speaks of passion and loyalty, I will speak of passion and loyalty. It's going to be tough. He has art and the spectra of a thousand digital boyfriends reinforcing him. I have only my bruised and lonely heart; have only the real world, with Venus missing.

Problem #3:
AT THE SCHILLER-OBERSCHULE

It is 1934 and you are the principal of the Schiller-Oberschule. You have received a directive from the *Reichsministerium für Volksaufklärung und Propaganda* that all students are to be instructed in the proper performance of the National Socialist salute. You are practicing it yourself in the mirror in your office. You are a little dismayed to see that the shoulder of your tailored suit bunches up whenever you perform the salute, but that is not the question before you. The question before you is what to do with the Jewish students—are they to be included in the lesson, or are they to be excused? The directive is unclear, saying in one place "*alle deutsche Studenten*" and in another "*alle Studenten in Deutschland*" which, as you see, leaves the question unsettled. You do not wish to be delinquent in your responsibilities in this matter but—damn that suit jacket!—but just what *are* your responsibilities?

THE MADONNA OF THE RELICS

He felt it most in the evenings. After a day of cleaning an archangel's silk or the Virgin's brocade he would let himself get lost in the fabulous city, walking beside the canals and over the arched footbridges, torturing himself with beauty. He would do his best to stay away from the tourists, keep from his sight the signs pointing to the Rialto or to San Marco, making his way instead through the darkening *calli* so exquisite with their rotting brick, the stone burned black with age. There was something to pain him everywhere he looked, something in every vista, every cul-de-sac: an unexpected belltower heaving into view, a salt-scarred aedicula empty of its Madonna—beauty everywhere, until at the end of the day, when the sun had set and the outdoor restaurants had come alive and his nerves were lit, there would be the women waiting for him.

They sat in twos and threes—Americans, Germans, Italians—or they sat with their boyfriends, their husbands, their lovers. He would stroll through the larger piazzas, the Campo San Polo or the Campo Santa Margherita, from restaurant to restaurant looking for the right one, and an empty table near her. When he found her he would seat himself—the waiters didn't care—and order in his not-bad Italian a half-liter of red wine, maybe some *crostini*. He was always discreet—part of the torture was to *not* look, to *feel* the woman near him: the allure of her hair, her neckline, the haze of her perfume—letting the wine burn its way into him before casually lifting his eyes or

45

turning in his seat to glance at her, whoever she was, with her beauty, her varnish, her impenetrability.

It was impossible for him to approach them. Even those rare times when he came upon a woman alone, someone near his own age, sitting like an invitation, he could not do it. It was not just a matter of not knowing what to say, or how to say it, or fearing that there was a delayed husband, a boyfriend about to return from the WC. No, it was that he had no talent for the physical. No talent for the life of the flesh. He knew this, knew that later—in some hypothetical future—he would be unable to reach out to her. He could *imagine* himself doing it—that was part of the pleasure: some painterly scene alongside a canal, the luxuriant green decay, a garland of lamplight, maybe a light drizzle and a black umbrella under which to kiss—but he knew, sitting there while the waiter brought his *secondo* (the candlelight on her collarbone!) he knew he could never touch her.

———

He had come to Venice three years earlier at the invitation of Aldo Manini, the director of the San Gregorio Restoration Laboratory. How long he would stay he didn't know—his salary, the technical research, even the heat to keep the lab open in winter: everything was dependent upon outside funding—but he had arrived with superb credentials and during his stay had impressed the Superintendency with his almost eerie ability to anticipate the chemical analysis and the results of infrared photography. Manini called him his American *wunderkind*. He was thirty-two.

The lab itself was housed in a deconsecrated church that backed onto the Grand Canal. The building was all that was left of the medieval abbey of San Gregorio. His current work— he had been at it for over a year—was the huge Carpaccio *Annunciation* from the Church of San Samuele: the Virgin with demure hand raised to ward off the archangel Gabriel who kneeled outside her bedroom window, the Holy Ghost a golden shaft about to pierce her heart. For the first eight months of the restoration the painting had lain face-down on the felt-covered floor of the nave while he and his assistants had crawled above it on cantilevered scaffolding, laboriously lifting rotting canvas and impacted dirt and a black fungus from off its back. From time to time tour groups came to watch: American college students, Germans, English, Italians from the Istituto Statale d'Arte. He did not like it when they were there, pretended when the Americans asked questions not to speak English; when the Italians did, not to speak Italian. His assistants at first wondered at him, then learned to answer for him. Later, when the painting had been stabilized and hung in the chancel studio, all visitors were kept behind a plexiglas wall through which they could gaze at the magnificent *Annunciation*, and at the solitary restorer with his back to them, cleaning, centimeter by centimeter, the painting's exquisite surface.

Oh, it was not lost on him—the irony of a man who was incapable of touching a flesh-and-blood woman, spending his day caressing a painted Virgin. The only man in the world—literally!—allowed to touch her. Nor was she the only virgin in Venice. Every campo had its church, and every church its Annunciation, its Madonna and Child, its Pietà. In his wanderings he would gauge the lovely faces against Carpaccio's, the slender bodices, the innocent hands held up in alarm, sorrow, acquiescence. He was in love with each, promiscuous with all, adored one's bare arms, another's faint bosom, a necklace, a pink toe peering out from under a hem. Oh, he knew you were not supposed to feel this way about the Virgin Mary! You were supposed to desire flesh, not spirit. Certainly not flesh got up as spirit. But there were worse abnormalities, weren't there? Whom did he hurt immuring himself in this rich sterility? A shy American art restorer, whispering to his Madonnas, standing on damp, consecrated stone and confessing his love to a young girl accosted by an archangel in the dead of night?

———

She had, after all, been a real girl first. Carpaccio's model, he meant. Some silk merchant's daughter or pretty orphan girl from the Ospedale, dressing up in rich robes, pretending. She had lived in the very city he lived in. She had known its fetid air, its tides, its courtyards with their spangles of sun. Sometimes he would pick out a stone, an old sill or a lintel and think how she, too, must have seen it, passed by it—who knew?—perhaps every day. Why some obscure piece of stonework spoke to him more than picturing her in front of, say, the Doge's Palace or inside San Marco, he couldn't have said. Except that everyone saw those; there was nothing of the intimate in them, whereas in the out of the way, in the privacy of the inconsequential— there, he felt, they could meet.

So when he saw her that day—not *her* of course, not Carpaccio's model, but *her*—it took him by surprise. It was summer and he had gone inside the basilica to get out of the heat, and then into the tiny rooms of the Treasury to get away from the tourists. He was going from display case to display case, gazing at the golden chalices and the gem-encrusted crucifixes, when a group of college students came in. They were Americans, dressed in shorts and tanktops, one of the girls in a minidress. "Gross!" he heard from the adjoining room where the reliquary cases were, and when the others had jostled their way in: "Is that, like, his *real* arm?" He tried to concentrate on the silver coffer before him. It was Byzantine, circa 1230, studded with emeralds and a single ruby. "That is *so* gross!"

And then they were gone. He moved to the next case, and the next, and then stepped into the room where the relics were.

Well, he had to admit, there *was* something gross about it. He had been brought up Baptist and this adoration of the flesh, of the horrific sufferings of saints, had baffled him when he'd first come to Italy. Even now, accustomed to seeing the fingers, eyeballs, the toes and tongues of saints encapsulated in silver and gold, he still felt removed. He could never quite shake the

Protestant's doubt. And yet lurking behind that doubt was the feeling that he was missing out on something, as though his skepticism was a kind of colorblindness, and the rich hues that others could see—these Italian nuns in their black dress, with their rosary beads and miraculous medals—were invisible to him, and that his world was paler, cooler, for it.

When he turned from the display case it was just in time to see a young girl kiss a small crucifix on a chain and press it against the glass of the case next to him. It took him a moment to understand what she was doing, that she was presenting, *exposing*, the crucifix to the relic. She had closed her eyes, as if to help conjure into the silver cross whatever thaumaturgic power was in the relic. He knew he should look away, move away, pretend to be admiring something else. But he couldn't, couldn't even when the girl opened her eyes and started at being watched. She shot a look at him and then, embarrassed, perhaps angry, closed her fist around the crucifix and let her hand drop to her side. She stood a moment longer in front of the display case, coloring under his gaze, and then quickly left the room.

He hadn't meant that. He hadn't meant to trespass like that—it was just that he had been taken so by surprise. And moved: how beautiful it was, what she had done! For a moment he had the urge to hurry after her, to apologize. But he stayed where he was, let enough time elapse for her to get away, and then went back into the nave. But he knew, even as he held back, that he was looking for her.

And she was there, in the crowd, gazing up at the mosaics on the domes overhead. He kept his distance, pretending absorption in this or that artwork. He did not, after all, want to be a creep. He only wanted to watch her, marvel at her.

And then—oh!—she saw him. He was far enough away so it was not incriminating, but she seemed again to fluster, to put her head down and move away. He stayed along the far aisle, lingering before the Mascoli Chapel, and then the reliefs surrounding the Porta dei Fiori, keeping his back to her but managing to turn around from time to time in mock abstraction. When he noticed her heading for the atrium and the doors that gave onto the piazza, he couldn't help himself, he followed.

There were girl friends, two of them, waiting for her in the piazza. He had thought she was maybe fifteen or sixteen—she was small, slight, breastless—but these others were older. College students, he thought. American maybe, or German. They stood with their hips cocked, their midriffs bare. They had beautiful, unruly hair, both of them. By contrast the girl with the crucifix was plain, unsure, in hip-huggers that didn't hug. Her friends closed around her—she was evidently telling them something—and then shot a look over their shoulders up at the atrium doors. But he was back, inside the shadows.

It was tricky, keeping the right buffer of tourists between them. Too large and he might lose her, too small and he would be seen. They left the piazza and headed down the Merceria. From time to time one of the girl friends turned her head, as if on the lookout. And once, he thought a breach in the sightseers gave him away. But they didn't stop. He followed them past San Zuliàn, across a canal and into the Campo della Fava. There they stopped on the steps of the church and he had to turn aside, feign interest in a shop of Mardi Gras masks. There was the long beak of the Plague Doctor, the open lips of Columbine. When after a minute he judged it safe to turn around he was shocked to see them staring straight at him, the two friends, startled as well to see that she was no longer with them. It took him another instant to realize that she was not ten feet away, advancing on him with a look tremulous and angry.

"What are you doing?" she said in terrible Italian. "Get away from me!"

"*Signorina!*" he said, sounding ludicrously gallant even in his own ears. He switched to English, thinking she was American.

"I'm sorry," he said.

"Leave me alone!" she said in accented English. German? Dutch? "I'm not bothering you. You go away."

"Please," he said. He lay his hand—what was he doing?—over his heart. "I'm sorry."

"We'll call the police!"

"It was only that you were so beautiful," he said. "What you did. It was so beautiful!"

She blanched, stared wordlessly at him. The girl friends were still throwing him dirty looks.

"It was so beautiful," he found himself saying again. "It moved me."

Her lips quivered. Her eyes glistened.

"I'm sorry!" he said. His hand was still over his heart. She let out a little gasp. "But you were so beautiful."

"No!" she cried. She began backing up. "No!" she said and spun around, hurrying back to her friends. This time, he had the good sense to let them go.

———

And then something he could not explain happened. Back up on his scaffolding the next day, working in the upper corner where the dove of the Holy Ghost had left a trail of fluttering gold in its earthward flight, he grew aware of someone watching him. In truth there were dozens watching him, a tour group from one of the istituti, but this was something else, something more than just an aggregate stare. He felt, in the back of his head, the insistence of someone's gaze. He had long been in the habit of never turning around when a tour group was there, but now he couldn't help himself. Beside him the archangel Gabriel kneeled with his terrible news. He closed his eyes, and then, pretending to need something from his tool caddy, turned.

And there she was. On the other side of the plexiglas, her face tense with wonder. They were looking straight at one another, as if each meant to ask the other how—with the hundreds of thousands of people in the city—how this could be. For ten or twelve seconds there was between them an abrupt and leveling intimacy. And then the tour leader raised his flag and the group began to move away. She cast her eyes about in confusion. One of her friends came over to her, took her by the arm, led her away.

He thought for a moment that he would go after her, place himself in the nave somewhere so that when the group came out of the chemistry lab he could step forward, signal her, let her know somehow that he wanted her. And then it would be her choice. That was how it was done, wasn't it? And yet he stayed where he was, two feet off the ground, a beaker of distilled water in his hand—

Ten minutes later when he heard the shuffle of the tour group on its way out, he was back at work, his face not six inches from the wall of paint, measuring color, value, hue. He didn't stop until he was certain she was gone.

He had after all, as he put his materials away, his evening ahead of him, the maze of the *calli* to lose himself in. There would be his virgins to visit and when the outdoor restaurants lit their candles, the women waiting for him. He changed out of his smock, out of his work shoes and into his street shoes, said *ciao* to Manini, to the others, and headed for the door.

She was waiting for him. Small, tense, her legs drawn together, she was sitting in a niche-like stoop tucked into the building across the way. At the sight of him she rose, brushed the seat of her pants. She said "hello" with a nervous smile, and he realized with amazement how he must appear to her: a man with an important job, an interesting life. He had taken a few steps toward the Campo della Salute when he'd come out of the building, and now she drew up to him. Her girlfriends were nowhere to be seen.

He didn't know what to say, didn't in fact say anything but turned to the piazza and the broad water at the mouth of the

Grand Canal. Then he filled the silence by pointing out the Palazzo Gritti where Ruskin had lived, and the Palazzo Giustinian where Turner had stayed. And there was Desdemona's house—did she know *Othello*? She looked intently up at him and didn't answer. And then, as if to let him know that she did not mean to have her feelings turned aside, she reached for his hand.

"Don't touch me," he said before he could stop himself. He thought he could see the irises of her eyes shrink. She backed away, and her thin frame seemed to tremble. Around her neck, falling inside her blouse, was the silver chain of her crucifix.

"In Venice—" he said, and he held out his own hand, caressed the air between them, but no more—"we don't touch, we look."

———

Her name was Lisette. She was nineteen. She was studying literature at Leiden and had come to Italy because she had read Dante in Dutch and then in English, and each time she felt like she wasn't getting it. So now she was in a language immersion course at the Istituto Venezia. Her girlfriends were not really her girlfriends. They were just roommates. They had only known her for three weeks but considered it their job to protect her from herself.

She was, he thought, sitting across from her that first evening in the restaurant, the day's heat still in the brick underfoot, an odd little thing. There was her too-big nose, her tiny teeth like immature kernels of corn, her bitten nails, her frightened eyes. And how pale her skin was!—he could see the veins in her temples, on the undersides of her forearms. And yet she seemed wonderfully alive to the world, painfully alive, as if the everyday sensations of living—the drifting perfume, the sunlight dying on the ochres of the campo—as if all this pleased and pained her in equal parts. By the end of the evening he found himself—in his own way—half in love with her.

And so there began, in the days that followed, a romance he grew to think of as a courtship of souls. She took him to hear

Vivaldi; he showed her his virgins. Where before he had been alone in the midst of the shimmering city, now she was there. She never tired of looking, of judging the proportions of, say, these quatrefoils as against those, of turning down some dark *calle* to see what was there, and when it dead-ended, turning around and going down another. She was strangely—to him, beautifully—moved by the empty embrasures they happened upon, the niches that had once held a saint or a Christ child and which now were vacant. When in a *scuola* or a church he showed her one of his favorites she listened intently to him, as if she might find some answer to what pained her in the violet shadows Tintoretto had painted into some saint's robes. He would incline his head to her and whisper, and the closeness of her skin, of her luminous eyes and the taut stretch of her pale throat, would make the room swim.

She never mentioned, and he never brought up, the zippers of scar-tissue on the undersides of her wrists.

Without alluding to the change in their lives, they began to go everywhere together. She was on a program of attending Mass in every church in the city—San Sebastiano one week, San Martino the next—and so he began to accompany her, seating himself on her far side so that he had a view across her of the priest celebrating mass, could watch her strained and intent face as she spoke the liturgy. They went to concerts at the Scuola di San Rocco and the Pietà. On weekends they took a vaporetto to the lagoon islands, watched the glassblowers in Murano, hiked along the silted canals on Torcello. At the Protestant cemetery on San Michele they searched out the graves of Stravinsky and Diaghilev—and how touched she was by the toe-shoes someone had left atop Diaghilev's tombstone!

Sometimes—he didn't mean for it to be cruel, only to add its own dark tint—he recounted for her the stories of forbidden love that had Venice as backdrop: the middle-aged Aschenbach gazing at his young boy on the verandah of the Hôtel des Bains,

Ruskin in old age returning to Venice to grieve for Rose La Touche. And there was the innocent, full-souled, tragically ill Milly Theale splendidly loving the worthless Densher. From atop the Campanile he pointed out the storied palaces, the curtained windows behind which passion had spent itself three and four centuries earlier. He showed her the rooftops over which Casanova had escaped from prison, pointed to this and that palazzo where the marvelous seducer had unclothed some nobleman's daughter, some merchant's wife. And the nuns he had debauched: the mysterious M.M. of the *Memoirs* and the innocent C.C. immured by her father in the convent of Sant'Angelo, whom the thirty-year-old Casanova had possessed in the convent chapel. And then he would speak to her of the Italians' talent for the flesh, their way of painting the flesh as if it were wine they were rolling in their mouths—until he could feel her, in the humid evening, growing moist beside him.

And then, one August night, he made an error. They had come out of the Pietà after a concert and were walking along the broad Riva degli Schiavoni. It was ten o'clock but the fondamente was still filled with tourists. As they walked he pointed out the house where James had written parts of *The Portrait of a Lady*. A little further on they paused to look at the Bridge of Sighs. And then as they started to cut across San Marco she had an idea. Why not take a gondola? She looked up at him with her face suddenly girlish. She had never been in one, she said, and she was leaving in ten days—why not take a gondola back to her room! Afterwards he would wonder why he hadn't been more careful. But it was so public there in the great piazza, with the schmaltzy sound of piano music carrying over the rows of outdoor tables, and behind them the gondoliers loafing and smoking cigarettes around the foot of the columns. They turned and headed back toward the rank of gold and black boats moored to their piles. One of the gondoliers in his striped shirt and beribboned hat hurried toward them.

"A gondola ride for the lovers!"

If he had been alone, he would have turned away. But together they hesitated, as if each meant for the other to decline.

"I have the good muscles," the gondolier said and he smiled at Lisette. "I take you anywhere!"

In as formal Italian as he could muster he told the man that he was taking the *signorina* home, that she lived in Dorsoduro, near the Ponte dei Pugni.

"Si, *si!* I take you." And he gestured with his hand toward one of the boats. "But round and round first, yes?" And he looked for an okay from Lisette. "We go deez way, we go dat way! Si?" And he made in front of her a slalom motion with his hand. She smiled her shy, pained smile and said "*si.*"

At first it wasn't so bad. They sat on the plush seat with the gondolier standing at his rowlock behind them, and there was enough bustle—the water taxis making their way up and down the Grand Canal, the souvenir sellers along the fondamente— that they were not so aware of what they were doing. But when they turned into one of the narrow canals, left the sweep and tumult of the Grand Canal behind, then the expectations of a man and a woman in a gondola together began to assert themselves. Was he not supposed to put his arm around her? Was she not supposed to lay her head on his shoulder? And this bridge coming up, when the gondolier gave his strong stroke and stooped as they glided under it, was he not supposed to lift her face to his and kiss her on the lips? He could feel her beside him thinking the same thing, her hands hugging her elbows as if she wanted to shrink into herself.

It was horrible. They kept their eyes averted, didn't speak. He could sense the gondolier behind him, feel his eyes on him, derisive—didn't these Americans know how to love? From time to time they had to steer to the side of the canal and let another gondola pass. With each new gondolier, with each pair of lovers, the space between them grew colder. He tried to concentrate on the city itself, the churches and the jeweled lights, all the sights they had loved, and yet it was as though the beauty had turned on him, had revealed itself as—he didn't know how else to say it—as *expectant*. He had the queer feeling of being presented with a bill for what he had thought was free.

"So what's wrong with me?" he heard whispered beside him. He turned his head to the small, strange woman. She was peering into her lap.

"What?" he whispered—had he heard right?—"What did you say?" But she didn't repeat it, only turned her face away. He gazed at the back of her head, at her hopelessly plain hair, and he knew then that he had been terribly wrong. That she had been fragilely waiting for something he had never intended to give. He shifted away and stared blindly at the dampcourse that ran along the edge of the canal. Ahead of them a group of teenagers was horsing around on a bridge—baseball caps, a Nike sweatshirt. The gondola slid under the bridge and came out the other side.

"Dude! Give her a feel!"

He would have to explain. When they got out of the gondola and he walked her to her room as he had so many other nights, he would explain. She was leaving in ten days, he was thirteen years older, how could there be a future? They had had beautiful moments, he would always remember her—the Madonna of the Relics!—he would always remember the way they had loved the city together. He would explain. They were excuses, he knew, but they would sound like the truth. At least he would spare her feelings.

But when they reached the Ponte dei Pugni and the gondolier had brought the boat alongside a mooring, she got to her feet and without waiting to be helped—"*Signorina!* Careful!"—stepped out onto the fondamente and began walking hurriedly away. He stood up in the rocking boat and called her name, but at the sound of his voice she began to run. Her heels made a hard, nightmarish sound on the paving. After a dozen yards the *calle* turned and she was out of sight.

"*Signor*," the gondolier said, embarrassed.

There was nothing to do but to thrust his head down, get out his wallet, pay the man.

"*Grazie, signor*. She is okay?"

But he had already started down the *calle*. He didn't hurry, but when he had turned the corner and made it out of sight, he stopped. He stopped, sat down and closed his eyes.

There was God looking down from the clouds as if from out of a window; there was the stream of gold flying from Him toward the Virgin's heart; and there was the Archangel Gabriel kneeling in the street outside her window. He had all along thought the discoloration of the angel's wings, the faint brown that tinged their tips, was an effect of the re-varnishing the painting had been subjected to in the nineteenth century. But he had cleaned it of that varnish, and of the retouching that had been done over the years, and yet the discoloration had remained. He had turned to chemical analysis, infrared- and micro-photography, under a raking light had looked and looked for signs of spurious correction. But he could find none. The yellowed, earthy color of the wingtips seemed worked into the paint.

He would leave her alone. It was what he decided the next day, back at work, puzzling over the archangel's wings. What he had done, or not done—if she didn't understand then it couldn't be explained. What excuse could he give? That he loved her soul but had never intended to love her body? And yet how odd it was! Because you *ought* to be able to say that to someone. If people were what they said they were—soul, spirit, heart, mind! But when he imagined going to her, all he could see in his mind's eye was her hurt, her rejected body. That wan face, the nervous throat, the faint swell of her bosom—untouched, unloved.

When four o'clock came, he put his gear away as he always did, washed up, said *ciao* to the others.

He half-hoped, half-feared she would be waiting for him in her usual spot, the stoop where she had been that first day. But the embrasure was empty. He took the traghetto across to the Gritti and tried to resume his old ways, going from *calle* to *calle*, turning after a while into San Samuele where for five centuries Carpaccio's *Annunciation* had hung. In the damp church he stood before a blank wall and read—queerly, as if trying to reassure himself of who he was—that the painting had been removed for restoration. Then he turned around to the great space of the nave. It was here, he remembered telling Lisette, that a youthful Casanova had drunkenly botched his duties and was obliged to leave the priesthood. Casanova, a priest! And they had laughed—

When the sun began to set he started his search. He kept to his favorite piazzas, pretended indecision over this woman, that woman, chose finally—it was getting late—a young beauty in summer yellow: spaghetti straps taut over her collarbones and a boyfriend in a rugby shirt. He took up his position, ordered a *mezzo* of wine, some *crostini*, teased himself with not looking. It would be all right. He would restore his life. In a minute, he would turn, he would look, he would touch her with his eyes. In a minute—

But he could not rouse himself, could not seem to care whether this woman with her rugby-playing boyfriend felt the obscure kiss of his soul or not. And when the waiter came to take his order, he found he had no heart to eat. He ordered another *mezzo* instead, sat and watched as the dusky bustle of the campo drained into night. When the man and woman rose to go he did not follow them as he usually did. He drank, slouched in his seat, tried—weirdly, drunkenly—to hold as still as he could, as if he were a figure in a painting, his body coated with varnish. The waiters began putting the chairs atop the tables around him.

Ten minutes later he was making his way over the crumbling bridges and through the slanting alleys which he knew would never again look the same to him.

It was one of the roommates who answered his ring. She came down the narrow, tilting, ill-lit stairway, opened the street door and at the sight of him scowled.

"She doesn't want to see you," she said before he could speak.

"Please," he managed.

"We spent a terrible night with her. A terrible day. She's only just managed to fall asleep."

"I'd like to see her. I'd like to speak with her."

She shook her head, stood there like a sentry. She was lovely, could have been one of his restaurant women.

"I want to help her."

"It's *you* who needs help."

He bowed his head, acknowledged the force of what she said. "Perhaps she and I—" and he spoke the words into the dust at his feet—"perhaps we can help each other."

And then he heard, on the stairway, someone else coming down. He saw in the dingy light the familiar feet first, and then descending: her skinny knees, the boyish hips. She was wearing a short nightdress and her face was ragged with lack of sleep.

"Lise—" the roommate warned.

"It's all right," she said in a faint voice. She stepped onto the stoop in her bare feet but wouldn't meet his eyes. The roommate hesitated a moment, then grimaced and started back up the stairs.

They stood apart, unspeaking. She had her arms about her waist, elbows clutched in her hands. He could see in the dim lamplight the white weave of the scar-tissue on her wrists. He could tell from her face that she had been crying.

"Lise—" he began, but couldn't finish. She pursed her lips, peered at her knuckles.

"I know I'm not pretty."

She said this without looking at him. He felt a pang at the sight of her down-turned head, and yet he could not move, could not speak. "It doesn't matter," she said. She gave a short, bitter laugh, and then let her eyes drop to the stone stoop. "I'm hopeless at sex anyway."

There was, after all, nothing of Carpaccio's Madonna about her, nothing of the Virgins he loved. Neither the blond ringlets nor the calm acquiescence. She was just a girl, some Amsterdam businessman's daughter whom he had first glimpsed in an unreal moment, there in the Treasury, her body upstaged by that one incandescent, transfiguring gesture of her spirit. Yes, it had caught and held him. He had loved that young girl with the crucifix. But now he saw who she really was. She could not escape her body. He could not escape it. It stood there before him, barefoot on the dirty stoop, alive, begging to be touched.

And then it came to him—stupidly irrelevant!—that the discoloration in the archangel's wings had nothing to do with old varnish, spurious repainting, spores, mold, mildew. The wings had opened, closed, stirred the dust when the archangel landed, and they were now—how simple it was! how had he not seen before?—they were dirty. The dirt was part of the painting.

Above them a casement window opened, someone looked out, and then the window closed again.

What he felt when he reached out and touched her wrist was not the softness of her skin, or even the reality of her scars, but a rushing vibration in the unvarnished air, the flutter of wings, and when she raised her tear-stained face to his, a stream of gold about to pierce his heart.

Moral Problem #4:
HANNAN OF THE SUQ AL-BARRA

You were born in the village of the streams. Your father and your grandfather were charcoal-makers in the Jbalan highlands. Even today, though you have lived all of your young life in Tangier, they call you a Jibli, a person from the mountains.

There are two girls. They are both—strange, yes?—they are both named Hannan. There is Hannan of the cobblestone quarter and there is Hannan of the Suq al-barra. You are meant to marry the first Hannan—how lucky you are! people tell you, how good she is! how beautiful, her skin is white like milk!—but it is Hannan of the Suq al-barra who you cannot get out of your thoughts.

The brideprice for Hannan of the cobblestone quarter is two hundred thousand francs. Your stepfather cannot help mentioning this. He is proud that it is so much. She is the daughter of al-Hajj Murad Zillal who owns a tobacco store. He has educated her well and she has passed the exam for the *brevet* and is qualified to be a secretary. There is even talk that she may go on to the Ecole Régionale d'Instituteurs when, after a year, she will have the certificate to teach elementary school. If this happens, your stepfather boasts, her brideprice will be even higher.

You do not know what the brideprice is for Hannan of the Suq al-barra. There is no one to inquire on your behalf. It cannot be much.

62

You limit yourself to going every third day, walking after school up the Street of the Jewelers. To disguise your interest you usually buy some bread or *gwaz* and wander among the stalls, eating. You do it in such a way that it will appear that you have just happened upon the mother and daughter who sell coriander and parsley. Each day you pray that she will be there, because sometimes her mother sends her to the *muqaf*, the "standing place" where women offer themselves for menial labor. You are old enough to know that, for a poor girl, it is only a step from the *muqaf* to the bars of the Bni Yidir quarter.

She is not as pretty as the other Hannan. Her skin is dark and there is hair—like black cirrus clouds—along her cheeks. But her eyes have light in them. Her hips move like animals inside her *jillaba*. She smiles at you, laughs at you, ridicules your school jacket and tie. She calls your family the parsley-eating family. She arches her eyebrows as if daring you to claim her.

They live, you have found out, in a hut made of flattened oil drums in the eastern shantytown.

You go to your eldest stepbrother for advice. He is a *talib* and is known for his calm ideas. A Moroccan man does not fall in love with a woman, he says. To fall in love with a woman is to cause your manhood to leave you. His name is Si Ahmad Qasim. He has memorized the Quran. Go to the mosque, he tells you—he touches you kindly—go to the mosque and wash your heart.

You climb the Street of the Jewelers. You take off your tie on the way.

Her hair is black like charcoal. Her laugh is like a shooting star. When you hear the call to prayer coming over the rooftops it is to Hannan of the Suq al-barra you wish to turn, to her you wish to kneel. *Allahu akbar*, you whisper in penitence, *La ilaha illa Allah*, but it is no good. You cannot help yourself. Allah is in her hair, in her hips, in the hem of her *jillaba* dragging in the dust.

HANDS

Here in New England we sit in chairs.

It's from my porch rocker that I watch the raccoon. He usually comes at dusk, that time of day half dog and half wolf, when the downturned leaves seem to glow with the sunset and the upturned ones glimmer with moonlight. I watch him pad through autumn weeds while the sweat of my chair-making dries on my skin. He lingers in the shadows, still woodside, the sun falling further with each moment, and then waddles onto my lawn. He looks like a house cat once the woods are behind him. He tosses a wary look at me and then slowly disappears behind the chair shop. After another minute I hear the crash of my garbage can lid falling on the stones. He doesn't even bother to run off as he used to, dawdling at the wood's edge until it's safe to come back. He seems to know I won't leave my chair.

"A twenty-two," my neighbor Moose says while I pare stretchers. "A twenty-two and then we won't blow the bejesus out of the pelt."

I take a few more cuts with my gouge and then ask him how he thinks the raccoon has missed his trap line all this time. He peers at me with the cold menace of old age. He has a white beard that rims his chin like frost.

"It probably don't run my way," he says. "But if you want it trapped I can trap it. It's just easier to shoot it if it's coming every night like you're ringing the dinner bell. Right here," he says and he goes over to the window just above my workbench and taps at a pane. His fingers are scarred with patches of old frostbite. "We'll take this here pane out. I can rest the barrel on the mullion. If it's close enough I'll get it clean through the head and I'll be richer one pelt and you'll be poorer one dinner guest."

I tell him I'm not sure I want to kill him.

"*Him?*" he says. "How d'you know it's *a him?*" And he spits on my woodstove so the cast iron sizzles.

Outside, my moaning tree sends up a regular howl.

"*Please* cut that tree down, Smitty," my sister Jaxxlyn says every weekend when she comes up from New York. "It's driving me positively psychotic."

I tell her it's a poplar. I can't cut it down. I don't use poplar in my chairs.

"But you heat with wood," she says. "Don't you? Don't you heat with wood?"

Not poplar wood I don't, I say. Too soft.

"It's driving me positively psychotic, Smitty."

I say what about New York. What about the car horns and the sirens. She says they don't have trees that moan in New York, Smitty.

Smitty, she says.

My name is Smith. I'm a chairmaker with a tree that's grown itself tight around a telephone pole and a raccoon that's taken a fancy to my garbage. I've never minded the name Smith. I like the ancestral whiff of fashioning and forging in its single syllable. And I don't mind the moaning tree and its outrage over the telephone poles that have been stabbed into the landscape like stilettos, rubbing its insulted bark in the slightest breeze and howling when the wind blows in earnest. But the raccoon has unsettled me and I don't know why. My sister—who hates her last name and is being driven psychotic by my moaning tree—is not bothered by the raccoon.

"I think he's *cute*," she says, sitting on my porch with me as the fat creature moves from shadow into moonlight and back into shadow. "My friend Flora in the west seventies has a skunk for a pet. You should see him, Smitty! His little claws go clack-clack-clack on the linoleum, you know? Of course he's been desmelled or whatever they do to them. Oh!" she says as the garbage can lid crashes on the stony ground. "Isn't that the cutest thing? How does he do it? Just *how* does he do it? Do you leave the lid on loose for him? Is that how he does it?"

Hands, I tell her, and I feel a faint panic at the word. They've got hands. And I hold my own hands up in the gloom, the backs reddish with dusk, the palms silver with moonlight.

When Monday comes I try tying the lid shut with mason's twine. That night there is no aluminum crash and I think: so much for hands, so much for raccoons, so much for half dog and half wolf! The next day I start in on a set of eight Queen Anne chairs, carefully fairing the S-shaped legs to Hogarth's line of beauty. But that evening the raccoon comes trotting along the forest floor, hiking up onto my lawn behind the shop. It takes him a few minutes longer, but eventually the harsh, bright crash shatters the dusk. I sit in a stupor. In ten minutes he emerges from behind the shop trundling along. He pauses partway to the wood's edge and tosses me a scornful look over his shoulder and then vanishes into the now-dark bushes.

"You might open up a motel," Moose suggests, "seeing as what you already got yourself a rest'rant."

My cabriole legs aren't right. I can't strike the balance between knee and foot. It's never happened like this before. I get out Hogarth's *Analysis of Beauty* and look his S's over, and I print S S S S S on my graph paper, write my own name: Smith, Smith, Smith, Smith, but when I go to draft my Queen Anne leg I can't balance the knee to the foot, the foot to the knee, the S's top orb to its bottom. I spend a whole day at my drafting table, trying, and end up tossing a sheaf of rejected legs into the stove. That night the raccoon dines on pumpkin and old cantaloupe.

———

I get my bucksaw and my knapsack and my spool of pink ribbon. If I can't work I'll hunt wood, do the felling now and wait until the first decent snow to find the marker ribbons and sledge the logs out with Moose's snowmobile. I plan on a two-day roam, bringing my sleeping bag and some food. At the sight of my bucksaw, my moaning tree groans.

I'm going to forget about raccoons.

I poach my lumber, and maybe that's why I have a feeling of trespassing when I go into the woods, of being where I only half belong. There are stone walls everywhere, built in earlier centuries and now running mute and indecipherable through the forest. Walking, I try to picture perfect S's in the air, but the stone walls distract me. They are like hieroglyphs on the land. From time to time I come across an old foundation, a sprinkle of broken glass in the weeds and a small graveyard a ways off. I find a bottle or two, an old auger, but they look as alien there as I do. Farther on, the stone walls are so tumble-down they have ceased to look like walls. There is a feeling of low menace all around.

I mark my wood as I go, but on this trip I keep my eyes open for hollowed trees, for trees with holes, a cicatrix, disease. I climb up several and look inside, peer up the trunk of one, but there's no sign of habitation. That night, lying on dark pine needles, I have a recurring picture of the raccoon back at my house, sitting at the kitchen table in one of my chairs, with knife and fork in hand—perhaps a napkin—eating.

By noontime on the second day I've swung around to where I know there's a stand of tiger maple near a marshy pond two miles from the house. I spend the afternoon carefully harvesting the rare, figured wood, dragging the de-limbed trunks down to the pondside and stickering them off the ground so they won't rot. The work puts the raccoon out of my mind. I feel healthy, feel the steel teeth of my bucksaw sharp and vengeful, the rasp of the sawn wood like the sound of defeat. But after the last haul, just as I sit content and forgetful on a stump, I catch sight of a tiny footprint in the soft silt that rings the water. Farther on, there's another one.

There's a hush over the pond. The marsh reeds stand like pickets along the shore. Across the way the shadows between the junipers and low laurels seem to breathe in and out. I have a feeling of having been tricked, of having been watched all along.

On the water the whirligigs hover like spies. A scarlet leaf flutters through the blue air and lands a foot or so from the raccoon's footprint, then cartwheels slyly until it covers the print. But it's too late. In the west, where my house is, the sun is kindling nests of reddish fire in the blue tops of the spruces.

You've got yourself a comfy den, I'm saying half an hour later after I've found the raccoon's beech tree. I've brought a crotched branch from the pondside for a leg-up, and I'm peering into a yawning hole maybe ten feet off the ground. I say it out loud. I do. I say: leaves and dried reeds, decaying wood for heat, some duck down. You've done all right for yourself.

The trees seem to stir at the sound of my voice. I pull my head out and listen. They sound baffled, outraged. I want to say to them: "Do you think so? Do you think so? So I'm the intruder? Do you think so?" But I don't. I just look at the hasty illogic of the shadows. Trees don't come on all fours and pry your garbage can lid off, I say. Even Darwin can't see to that, I say, and I go back to looking inside the raccoon's den.

I'm not afraid he's in there somewhere. I *know* what time of day it is. I *know* where he is. But off to the side, in a decaying burl, something has caught my eye, something shiny and unnatural. I look closer and realize he's got himself a cache of junk, bottle caps and aluminum can rings. Then in the next instant I recognize a piece of old coffee cup I'd broken in the summer, and then, too, a router bit I'd chipped and thrown out, then an old ballpoint, a spoon, screws.

Are you a user of spoons, too, raccoon? I finally say out loud. And screws? And pens? Are you a writer of sonnets? I say.

But even as I talk I hear footsteps behind me on the leaves. I pull my head out and look around, but there's nothing moving, just the vagrant leaves falling. I listen again, hear them coming closer. Is it the raccoon returning? I hang fire a moment and then start hurriedly down the trunk. But before I do I reach in and steal back my old ballpoint. I hide the crotched limb in some bushes nearby.

— — —

For the next few days I wonder just how much the raccoon knows. There's no new contempt evident in his regard as he bellies up out of the woods onto my lawn—but he may be a master of his emotions. Jaxxlyn has put a bowl of water out for him. She says she's going to move it nearer to the house each day until the raccoon gets used to being with us. She wants me to do the moving on the weekdays.

My West Hartford client calls and asks how her Queen Anne chairs are coming. I start to tell her about the raccoon. I start to tell her about William Hogarth and beauty and order, about how a man can't work when a raccoon's eating his garbage, about how I've allowed eagle's claws for chair feet in the past, lion's paws too. But this raccoon is asking too much, I tell her. There's a silence on the line when I stop—and then she asks again how her chairs are coming.

"Six inches each day," Jaxx tells me as she gets into her car. "Six inches, Smitty."

Monday I can't work. Tuesday I can't either. Tuesday evening I wander off into the woods again, walk the two miles to the raccoon's tree. Somewhere on the way I know we cross paths. I get the crotched limb out of its hiding place and steal back a screw.

The next morning I get the mating S's of the cabriole legs down perfectly in ten minutes, and by sundown I have all sixteen legs squared up and cut. That night I take the router bit back.

Thursday it's another screw. Friday a piece of china. I'm going great guns on my chairs.

Jaxxlyn doesn't understand why the raccoon won't drink her water. She asks if I've moved it each day. Then she talks to the raccoon from the porch, talks to him so he pauses in his jaunty walk and looks our way. She alternates from a low, cooing voice to a high, baby voice. The raccoon and I exchange looks. He knows, I think to myself. He knows. He can hardly cart things off as fast as I can steal them back. He knows.

For the next week I am a maker of chairs in the daytime and a sitter of chairs at night. I'm a happy man. Only during the in-between hours do I venture through the woods to the raccoon's house and then venture back in the near-dark. I've taken to putting my booty back in the trash can.

My West Hartford lady drives cross-state to see how her chairs are coming along. I let her run her wealthy fingers across the soft wood, up and down the smooth legs. She shivers and says it feels alive still. "Doesn't it feel alive still?" she says.

Back in the woods I take a different route to the raccoon's tree. I figure I might catch him out this time, but it turns out we've merely switched paths, and he's trying to catch me out. I round the pond quickly, the last fall leaves floating like toy boats on the water, and hurry to the bushes where the crotched branch is hidden. The trees are quiet. I throw the crotch up against the tree-trunk, climb quickly up, and in the half-light see that the raccoon has taken the ballpoint pen back.

Still writing sonnets, raccoon? I say and reach for the pen. But just as I do the den bursts into a flurry of fur and claws and teeth. I hear a hiss, a growling sibilance, and just before I fall see two leathery hands gripped around my wrist and a furry mouth set to bite. An instant later I am lying scratched and hurt in the laurel below. Above me the raccoon peers fiercely down at me from his hole. His eyes are black and fanatical, and he seems to say: "All right? All right? Understand? All right?"

Violence! I spit through my teeth, stumbling back through the woods. I don't even try to stanch the blood coming from the punctures on my wrist. *Violence! Violence!*

———

Moose laughs. He laughs and asks how much the first of my rabies series costs. I'm sitting in his living room feeding bark into his stove. I don't answer him at first. I'm sick and I ache from the shot. Finally I tell him sixty dollars.

"Well, let's see," he says and he sights down the barrel of his twenty-two. "A raccoon pelt brings fifty dollar nowadays." He pantomimes doing sums in the air. "Means this here raccoon's a losing proposition."

The frostbite on his face crumples with his laugh, as if the skin there were half alive. I sit sullen and witless, wasted. The raccoon comes and ravages my garbage.

I lie in bed for two days. When I'm up again I ask Moose for one of his box traps. I tell him I don't want to shoot the raccoon, I want to trap him. And once I've trapped him I want to let him go. He looks at me like this is confirmation of some suspicion he's had about me all along, never mind raccoons, some suspicion he's had since he met me and my chairs.

"I ain't altogether sure a raccoon will trap so near a house," he says. "Raccoons ain't dumb."

This one will, I say. He's a modern raccoon.

But that night, sitting in my warm chair shop on a half-finished Queen Anne chair, I watch the raccoon stop and inspect the trap, puff at the acorn squash inside and then waddle over to the garbage can. He knocks the lid off with a professional air, but before he crouches into the garbage, he tosses a disdainful look through the windowpane at me and my chair. Behind him the trap sits in a state of frozen violence.

Beauty is the visible fitness of a thing to its use, I say to the raccoon in my dreams. Order, in other words. In a professorial voice he answers back: "Not entirely different from that beauty which there is in fitting a mortise to its tenon."

I wake in a sweat. My wound itches under its bandage.

On the second night, kneeling on the wooden floor in my shop, the chairs empty behind me, I watch the raccoon sniff a moment longer at the squash but again pass it up. This time it's contempt in his face when he catches sight of me through the windowpane. That night the air turns cold.

What do you want? I whisper to the raccoon in my sleep. *What do you want?*

"What do you want?" the raccoon whispers back. "What do you want?"

On the third night I forsake the chair shop for the junipers, hiding myself long before dusk in the green shrubbery that skirts the forest's edge. It's snowing. The flurries make an icy whisper in the trees overhead. I watch the sun fall through autumn avatars and set in blue winter. The snowflakes land on my eyelashes and melt New England into an antique drizzle. I blink my eyes to clear them and wait with my joints stiffening, my toes disappearing.

By the time the raccoon comes I am iced over, a snowy stump among the evergreens. He pads silently through the snow, leaving tiny handprints behind him on the slushy ground. He doesn't see me. I watch him with frost inside me, my breathing halted, my hands clubbed. He looks for me on the porch, in my rocker, then tries to spy me through my shop window. For an instant he seems stunned by my absence, by the change in things. He turns and peers straight across at where I sit in the frozen junipers. I am certain he sees me, even nod my head at him. For a moment we are poised, balanced, the one against the other. He blinks, acknowledging my presence in the snow, and then with an air of genteel reciprocation, turns and walks straight into the trap.

When I reach him he has his paws up on the trap's sides, the fingers outstretched on the fencing. He peers up at me as if to see if I'll take his hands as evidence after all. There are snowflakes on his eyelashes. When I bend over him our breaths mingle in the cold gray New England air.

Moral Problem #5:
HONI SOIT QUI MAL Y PENSE

You've just had the Big Argument and now she's gone. There have been many other arguments (you remember particularly the one about whether millionaire NBA players had the right to strike, a subject neither of you cared about in the least but somehow roused her outraged Jewish–IWW–Ellis Island sensibility against your snide Elitist–*Mayflower*–Wonder Bread privileged self), but this is the one that's going to do it. This is the one—about George-freaking-W.-Bush and the invasion of Iraq—this is the one that's going to sink the marriage before it even starts. She was arguing for Shock and you—of course—were arguing for Awe. Or maybe it was the other way around.

So you're sitting in the cafeteria of the Derby Technology Museum in Derby, England, from which she has just made her angry exit, trying to pretend nothing has happened so the others having their afternoon tea—the English from whom you are so snidely descended—will quit looking at you. You've got your she-just-had-to-go-to-the-loo look on, got your legs crossed in that feminine, elegant, handmade-Italian-shoes way you've practiced over the years, in and out of your two previous marriages, sitting there with your jaw set, calculating the likelihood of her being gone—really gone—when you get back to the hotel room. The rental car is in her name, you remember. You'll have to walk.

But to give her time to pack and clear out—if that is, in fact, what she's doing—you stroll back into the museum. You read again the placards that detail the building's history. An eighteenth-century silk mill whose founder was murdered for smuggling the plans for silk-throwing machines out of Italy. Nevertheless, you are pleased to be reminded, the Industrial Revolution marched undaunted on. Right up until today, when it began dropping millions of tons of explosives on Iraqi civilians.

You move on to a half-beam steam engine called the Grasshopper. Cylinder, side rod, flywheel.

In situations of this sort, the virtue of being the leaved instead of the leaver is that logistics are in your favor. It is the *leaver* who will have to change her plans. She can't expect to have the hotel room when you return to London—it's in your name anyway—and unless she wants to sit next to you for the seven-hour flight back to D.C., she'll have to change her plane ticket. You think of this with some satisfaction as you run your eyes over a steam-powered organ—*der Specht*, the Woodpecker—and then reach into your pocket and turn your phone off. If she tries to reach you, that'll only piss her off more.

When you step into the next room a strange sight awaits you. There's a Muslim woman there. A Muslim woman standing and looking at the bright, machined surfaces of a Rolls-Royce jet engine. She's dressed in full purdah—is that the right word?—black headscarf and robe: the whole deal although her face is not covered. You don't know what's weirder, her and the jet engine, or the fact that you and your fiancée had seen her the day before, at Chatsworth. There had been an older woman with her then. You are all, evidently, reading from the same guide book.

So you begin to follow her. Discreetly, of course. You mosey from exhibit to exhibit, employ strategies of coincidence and misdirection. The swaying garment, the suggestion of hips, of breasts, the wimpled face, the dark eyes—these are supposed to *not* arouse the baser passions, have you got that right? She stops in front of a glass case in which various scientific instruments are displayed. You sidle over to the cabinet and pretend to read one of the placards. She is, herself, dutifully studying each instrument. She moves toward the center of the display from the left—chronometer, altimeter—you move from the right—sextant, anemometer. In the center, there is an astrolabe, mysterious with its gold and silver, its delicate chasing. An hour earlier you and your fiancée had remarked on it, the pseudo-science of it, the attempt to rationalize the unknown. There are what appear to be astronomical symbols around the outside edge and in the central field—stars, planets, lines of cosmic latitude and longitude. You notice for the first time that the hands of the instrument are in the shape of fanciful serpents. Dragons maybe. Beside you the black hem of her gown eddies an inch above the floor.

"Imagine," you say, because this is the kind of mood you're in, "that something so medieval could survive into this century."

You have said this without looking at her. She neither acknowledges what you've said nor moves off. You wonder does she even speak English. A minute passes. It strikes you that you are both lingering too long over the object. After another minute, she speaks.

"Please?" she says in that Arab-English accent that is such a kick, "what does this mean?"

She is pointing through the glass to an inscription on the astrolabe. You had not noticed it before when you and your fiancée were looking at the case.

"Honi soit qui mal y pense," you read, and you know you should know this. It's a motto of the monarchy or something. You've got enough French to know that mal is "evil" and pense is "think," and you're pretty sure soit is the subjunctive of "be," but honi has got you stumped.

"It has something to do with thinking evil," you say. And

you like being able to say that to her. "It has something to do with a people thinking evil," you enlarge.

"I see," she says. And then: "Thank you."

Did she understand? you wonder. Shock and awe, hey? After another minute, she moves on. The older Arab woman that you'd seen the day before at Chatsworth—also in purdah—comes in from another room, joins the younger woman. They stop in front of the Woodpecker. Well, whatever. Fun's over.

Back at the hotel room, there is no shaving cream message on the bathroom mirror like in a bad movie, but neither is your fiancée there. The closet is cleaned out, as are the dresser drawers, the bathroom. She has, as a parting shot, left her diaphragm like a welcoming chocolate on your pillow.

Honi soit qui mal y pense, your laptop tells you, means "Evil to him who thinks evil." Well, you were close, you think as you look up and catch sight of yourself in the mirror on the back of the closet door. Which she left open no doubt to underline some point.

MISSING, BELIEVED WIPED

It was as if he had been there, with his parents and Speedy Alka-Seltzer and his nonexistent kid brother: in the den of their Levittown house, in front of the black-and-white Philco, with Ernie Kovacs and the dancing Lucky Strikes and outside the Fifties happening like a mushroom cloud.

Or in the turn-of-the-century tenements: say, this time, the Lower East Side with the smell of cabbage in the airshafts, the laundry strung from fire escape to fire escape, the pushcarts, the Yiddish, the rotting vegetables in the gutter, the tots singing "Ring-a-Rosie" and the fire at the Triangle still to come.

Or Main Street on a summer evening, the cars cruising past, Studebakers, Chevies, the T-bird her daddy had yet to take away: the soft Indiana night blooming, and him with his made-up buddies—Andy Carlson, Scooter McKane, The Douchebag—passing cigarettes and french fries and on the lookout for girls who never happened.

He lived in the patina of these things, in the surface glow of a past that was not his. LPs picked up from thrift stores, from eBay, advertising jingles downloaded in MP3 files. They had a heft that was lacking in his own life. He had only to see them, hear them, touch their worn surfaces and it was as though some archeology of his imagination uncovered in them—in the grass-stained baseball, in the mitt with the rotting stitching—drifting summer evenings, a halo of moths in the corner streetlamp.

Piece by piece he had shed his own life, dropped the subdivision outside Fresno where he'd grown up and adopted other, more iconic, origins: sometimes Levittown with its little prefab houses and struggling lawns and midget trees, other times the green ease of the Louisiana bayou, the windy blankness of Nantucket. Jazzman, Jew, whitebread kid from Muncie: who he was depended upon what he surrounded himself with, every inch of his NYU office covered with ephemera, postcards, advertising slogans, antique toys, bills, deeds. To pick one of them up—*Stalling Is Eliminated by Using Esso!*—was to have the rich vista of a past world open before him. By contrast anything from his own life, anything from 1975 onward, seemed impoverished, not quite there. Even the New York he'd found four years ago when he came to do graduate work had disappointed him. It had taken him months to begin to feel the antique under the modern, to see the ghosts of the garment runners on Hester Street, to hear the roar of the crowd that ran like rebar through the Ebbets Field Apartments. He began telling people he'd grown up in the East Village, had a pair of beatniks for parents. When September 11th happened he was thankful it wasn't the Chrysler Building or the Empire State. There had been no aura surrounding the World Trade Center.

His girlfriend of the time had taken that as the last straw. When she left, he put on his Guy Lombardo records and leafed through his copy of *The Saturday Evening Post.*

Ever since he'd been a boy he could spend whole days by himself. If he needed other people he found them in the statistics on the back of his baseball cards, or in his model railroad where August 8th, 1938 endlessly recurred (milkcans loading at the Central Dairy siding; No. 7 being rebuilt in the roundhouse). It was an empathy without consequences. There was the occasional actual person to indulge, nowadays his thesis advisor, the freshmen in his American Technostalgia seminar, the necessary girlfriend. He went to second-run movie houses with them, talked Barbie dolls and advertising slogans with the other Cultural Studies grad students, argued which came first, the Lucky Strike dancing cigarettes or the Kool dancing penguin? It passed for human interaction. Was sometimes more than he wanted.

So when the phone rang that day he didn't answer it. He never answered it, so this was no different. But the voice, half-heard from the living room after the answering machine kicked in, made him get up and walk into the kitchen to listen. He knew it was a wrong number—the emotion, the choking incontinence. Whoever it was, she was fighting to control herself. He stood there, embarrassed, unsure whether he should pick up the receiver and tell her she had the wrong number. And then she broke down, and for a good thirty seconds there was nothing but the sound of weeping. And then the sobbing turned into broken laughter, teary, maybe drunk. *Oh, god!* the voice said. She swallowed, swore, got herself under control. *Meet me at Daisy Buchanan's tonight, okay?* She sounded exhausted. *Denny? It's bad today. After work, okay?* And she hung up.

On the wall above the phone, his Felix the Cat clock wagged its pendulum tail.

It had to be because he never used a personal greeting, let the machine-generated voice welcome whoever called. She'd misdialed, didn't know she had the wrong number. He rewound the tape and played it from the beginning. *Pick up the phone, you insensible bastard.* He rewound and listened again, but that's what she'd said, not "insensitive" but "insensible." She called him Denny again. *It's me,* she said. She was at work. Could he call her? Could they meet? It was about the apartment. She wouldn't make a scene. But he was the only one who would understand. And then the crying began. And then the laughter.

For the rest of the morning he felt strangely haunted. It wasn't just the eavesdropping on another person's life, but an eerie sense that someone he didn't know was emotionally involved with him, was having her heart broken because of him, because of his coldness, his uncaring, his *insensibility*. He took the subway instead into Little Italy for a mid-morning espresso, stood at the polished bar and said "*prego*" and "*grazie*," pretended the cast brass and Gilded Age lettering was authentic. It helped. Back outside he gazed at the worn brick building fronts. In one of the railroad flats there was a door open and he caught sight of a stairway leading up to the second floor, the treads scalloped with a century of footsteps. He smelled garlic and oil cooking. He began to hear the sound of shod hooves on cobblestones. There was steam rising from the manhole covers. He walked and imagined himself with a Sicilian mustache.

Still, when five o'clock came he was outside Daisy Buchanan's in the West Village. He told himself it was because he didn't want her to think she'd been stood up. But he knew that it was something else as well, not simple curiosity, not quite voyeurism. She was a live piece of someone else's world. He could watch her. She might have some value.

He took up a spot at the bar where it curved toward the kitchen door. He could see the street from there, and most of the dining room. The restaurant had a twenties décor, with pictures of Robert Redford as Gatsby, Mia Farrow and Bruce Dern as Daisy and Tom Buchanan. Suspended from the ceiling were cloches and ostrich boas. And under the glass-topped bar, eighty-year-old front pages from the *Herald* and the *Mirror*. And some sports pages. But it was all merely decorative. It didn't live.

He knew, of course, that "after work" could mean midnight as easily as five o'clock. But he'd take that chance, wait an hour, see who showed up. He placed bets with himself on how old she would be, what she would look like. There was the question too of "insensible": was it ignorance or wit? He looked at each woman who came in—each of them accompanied by a boyfriend, a girlfriend, a husband—and measured her, practiced on her.

At quarter to six when she showed up, he knew her instantly. It was all there: the moment-before makeup, the controlled nerves, the scare that took over her face when the room didn't answer her look. She was maybe five years older than he was—thirty-three, maybe thirty-four—skinny in that nervous way some woman had, nicely dressed he supposed, an expensive-looking clutch under her arm. She spoke to the hostess and let herself be led to a small table over against the wall. When she passed the bar he turned casually away and positioned himself so that he could see her reflection in the mirror behind the bar. She shrugged her way out of her coat, let it drape behind her over the chairback. He hoped she wouldn't take out a book. That would be too sad.

Five minutes seemed the proper thing. He marked the digital numerals on the cash register, waited, watched. The waitress brought her—could she be so sure Denny was going to show up?—a whole bottle of wine. It threw his timing off. He had to let her drink a little, resettle herself. Then he stood up.

What he enjoyed most was the hardened look that came over her face when he stopped at her table. It was classic. It had provenance. He'd seen it in movies from the forties—very Barbara Stanwyck—that female barrier against a come-on. He smiled and didn't go away.

"Are you waiting for Denny?"

She flinched, drew back in her chair. "What?"

He smiled his Fred MacMurray smile. "You left a message on my answering machine. You must have misdialed."

Her brow clouded. It was going to take her a minute.

"You got my message?"

"Yes."

She raked his face with a look of mistrust. "What's your phone number?"

He told her.

"Nine three?" she said, repeating the last two digits.

"Yes."

She covered her face with her hands. And then there it was: the laugh he'd heard on his machine, choked, self-critical, but finding it funny just how awful things could be. The waitress brought a second wine glass, went away smiling at all the laughter.

"I'm *so* sorry," she managed to say, shaking her head at how stupid she could be. She wiped the laugh-tears from her eyes. "Please," she said, "sit down."

He sat down, waited for her to get herself under control. There was something wrong with her hair. It was longish, but very thin, with patches of wispy scalp showing here and there. She took a tissue out of her purse and blew her nose.

"God!"

Close up, she was sort of pretty, he supposed. At least there was a softness to her looks, something a little comical in the way her lips pursed. She had very small hands.

"You came all this way?" she said finally. "Just to tell me?"

He had the good sense to merely smile.

"That was very kind of you." And she gazed gratefully, a little in wonder, at him. "I'm Noreen," she said and held out her hand. "Or did I say that on the phone?"

It seemed to come to her as they shook hands what she had said on the phone, just how unmanned she'd been. She made a show of reaching for the wine bottle.

"Here," she said, pouring. "I was either going to get snockered with Denny or get snockered alone. Either way it was going to be the death of the old me and the birth of the new." She pushed a glass toward him and held up her own. "Here's to love."

"To love," he said, trying to inject some irony into the word, but she didn't bite. He took a drink, gazed out across the room, then let his eyes return along the wall. There was a photo of Coco Chanel above their table. "So who *was* the old me?"

She eyed him as if to warn him off trespassing. But then something of the self-lacerating tone he'd heard on the phone took over. "Someone who toasts to love," she said.

"And who's the new going to be?"

She drilled him with a look. "Someone who toasts to love."

This wasn't going right. He leaned back in his chair, tried to regroup. What had been the objective? He had wanted to see into another person's life. He had wanted to sit in a restaurant across from a woman who had been hurt, jilted, abused, and see her hurt, hear her accusations and her pleading. He had wanted to live in her life, *trespass* in her life, as he did when he imagined himself coveting the girl in the T-bird, running shirtwaists in the Lower East Side. He let his eyes drift away, over her head. *See the world today, in your Chevrolet!* he sang silently to right himself.

"You're looking at my hair," she said.

He recalled his gaze, smiled, shook his head *what?*

"It's all right." She pulled a strand in front of her eyes. "It's pretty ugly, I know. *Alopecia areata.* Another half a year I should be completely bald." She gave a little tug and the strand of hair gave way. She held it delicately between thumb and forefinger. "That's a good reason to dump a girl, isn't it?"

This was more like it. He assumed a solicitous pose. "Was that what Denny did?"

She shrugged.

"Boyfriend?"

She let the strand of hair fall to the floor. "Husband," she answered in a flat voice. "Ex." The waitress came, asked if they were ready to order, but she waved her off, said they would just have the wine. "You'll help me with this?" she said, pouring for him again. "Or do you have to go?"

He made an empty-handed gesture: his time was hers. She

put the wine bottle down, drank and then poised her wine-glass at her lips.

"So who are you," she asked, "with all your lucky hair?"

He paged through an index of selves. Who to choose? Who to be for her?

"Who am I?" he repeated.

"You have to think about it?"

So he told her, straight: an NYU graduate student, finishing his dissertation, teaching a course in pop culture. Unmarried, unspoken for, a Brooklyn Dodgers fan. She asked him what his dissertation was on and he told her: a semiotic reading of Levittown (A what? she laughed), well, more than that: the golden arches, Ebbets Field, Donna Reed's pearls: signs, symbols, the American pop landscape as hieroglyph. He was doing for tract housing what the nineteenth-century luminists had done for Niagara Falls. Which was what? she wanted to know. He was finding living meaning in the landscape, *creating* meaning out of the American Image. Out of the long-gone airwaves, out of the ephemeral, the vanished. It was fun. She peered at him with an intensity that puzzled him.

"Has anything really awful ever happened to you?"

The question took him aback. "Awful?" he wanted to know.

"Awful," she repeated and let the word stand on its own.

He told her no, he didn't think so.

"You don't think so?" she repeated, a little hostile.

"Other than growing up in Levittown," he laughed. Then, when she didn't play along: "No. Nothing really awful has ever happened to me."

She pressed her lips together, kept herself from saying anything more. Fragile, handle with Johnsons, he let the announcer in his head say. She drew back in her seat, as if from the edge of her rudeness, let her gaze drift around the restaurant. On the wall across the way was Gatsby's yellow Mercedes. This, he decided, still smarting a little, had been "their place." She and Denny meeting here to discuss whether he should accept the offer from Merrill Lynch. And that marvelous winter night—it was sleeting, remember?—when she had told him no, no alcohol for her tonight, because—guess! couldn't he?—she was pregnant!

"I have to go," she said, turning back to him.

So that was going to be it.

"Wait," he said. He searched for something with which to stall her. "Has anything really awful ever happened to *you*?"

The Barbara Stanwyck look came back. "You mean worse than my hair falling out? Worse than my husband leaving me?" Was he supposed to answer that? "You mean like breast cancer? Or my only child dying in a freak accident?"

"Forget it," he said. Then, defensively: "You asked me first."

She reached for her jacket on the chair back behind her, but then her shoulders slumped. She let the jacket puddle in her lap. "I'm sorry," she said. "It's a bad time for me. It's been a bad year."

"Tell me," he tried.

She shook her head "no," and then, as if to make it up to him: "But let's finish the wine. And you can tell me about the travails of growing up in—where was it?"

So half an hour later they were cutting through Washington Square on the way to his office to see his Levittown stuff. They stopped in front of the statue of *Washington at Peace* because he wanted to tell her—he'd been showing off his American Image repertoire since they'd left the restaurant—that the bodybuilder Charles Atlas had modeled for it back in 1918. If she stood right here—here, he said, touching her on the shoulders and orienting her—she could simultaneously *see* George Washington and smell the back pages of pulp magazines where the muscled photo of the World's Most Perfectly Developed Man had appealed to generations of 98-pound weaklings. Could she smell it? No? Well, *he* could! And he grinned at her, maybe a little drunk.

Inside his office while she looked at his Levittown adver-

tising circulars, he lectured her on how this was the original tract housing, the prototype for a subsequent America,
and how he'd grown up there (in the fifties, he almost said,
but caught himself), if not in the first wave of baby boomers,
well, later. He showed her on an aerial photograph the actual
house, the swingset in the backyard, maybe even that grainy
splotch his tousled self sitting on the teeter-totter. There were
dozens of books written on Levittown—he swept a hand at his
bookshelves—but they were all filled with the usual statistics,
graphs, postwar pie charts. He was after something quite different, something that married the flesh and the spirit, that
fused the pre-fab physicality of Levittown with the voiceover
that told you that in the sixty seconds this message took, Buff-
erin could already be in your system, fighting your headache.

"Yikes!" she said, rolling her eyes like who's the nutcase. He
smiled, ran a proprietary eye over the aerial photo, then looked
back at her.

"You'll wonder where the yellow went—"

And he took out the bottle of bourbon his office-mate kept
in a file cabinet, poured for her, for himself.

And tried to show her what he meant, the correspondence,
the mapping that linked the Levittown Tigers and the Esso
mascot. He got out his files and folders, played his DVD of
black-and-white advertisements, but as he talked he noticed
that she was distracted, that she kept looking sidelong at a
conference poster he had hanging on the inside of his office
door. When she became aware that he had stopped talking,
she laughed, apologized, then pointed at the poster and asked
what that was—*Missing, Believed Wiped*—what did that mean?

"It's a phrase the networks use," he told her. He shut the
DVD player off. "It's how they classify missing programs."

She gazed at him, then returned to the poster.

"Videotape was reusable," he explained. "So all these great
programs were purged, taped over. Don Larsen's perfect game

MISSING, BELIEVED WIPED 87

in the 1956 World Series. James Dean playing Jesse James in an episode of *You Are There. Esso Newsreel, Camel News Caravan*—all lost. Wiped."

"Wiped," she repeated out loud. There was something pained—was she just drunk?—in her expression. She reached her hand out to the poster, ran her fingertips over a photo of Ernie Kovacs.

"Except they're not."

She inquired with her eyebrows.

"They were broadcast, so they're all out there somewhere. Radio waves. In the universe somewhere—*The Kate Smith Hour, Treasury Men in Action*—they still exist, they're still alive, if you have the antenna to receive them."

He had meant it wryly—or at worst as a brag on the antenna that *he* had—but the look she gave him made him feel like she thought he was mocking her, making fun of some private hope—her husband? her hair?—some restoration that had been awakened by the odd phrase: if something was only *believed* wiped, then perhaps it wasn't.

"Are you all right?" he brought out at last.

"I've got to go," she said. She tucked her head in, didn't look at him. "I've got to get home to my daughter."

She opened the office door. He followed her out into the hall, nonplussed. "You have a daughter?"

But she didn't answer, didn't even turn. She walked down the hall, into the stairwell. He had to turn and lock the door, then hurry to catch up. Out on the street he thought he heard her say, under her breath, "*wiped*" but when he shot a look at her, her lips were closed. He did his best to keep pace with her. They were headed downtown, toward SoHo. It was eight-thirty, maybe nine o'clock.

"James Dean—" she said suddenly when they were nearing Houston; he had been just about to give up, be discreet, leave her alone—"Charles Atlas!"

She kept her eyes straight ahead, but her face was gripped with emotion. He didn't answer. They crossed Houston. Five minutes went by. Then:

"You think you can smell the back pages of comic books!"

She seemed on the verge of crying, of losing it like she'd done on the phone. He didn't know what exactly she was talking about, what it was that had so distressed her. Still, he kept alongside her. They turned down Mercer Street. The pedestrians thinned out.

"You're pretty upset," he said finally. "Perhaps I should go."

On either side of them there were warehouses with cast-iron facades. Victorian Gothic, Italianate, neo-Grecian. He could tell her all about them, make the skivvy-shirted laborers live for her. Did she not want that?

"I'll leave you alone."

But she kept walking, gave him no opportunity to leave except rudely. A yellow cab zoomed past. Then—oddly, unexpectedly—she took his arm.

"I want you to meet Abbie."

"Abbie?" he repeated. "Your daughter?"

Her face eased, relaxed.

"How old is she?" he asked, for something to say, but she was someplace else. Gone was the fierce emotion that had got hold of her. Something, some thought, had calmed her. In another instant she closed her eyes and—trusting him to look out for her—walked a good thirty yards blind. There was the faintest smile on her lips.

"Listen . . . ," he began to say, but she had stopped, opened her eyes.

"There," she said, as if she were soothing someone. "I'm all right now." She turned something like her old face on him. "You'll come up for a minute?" And she climbed onto a loading dock that ran along the building they were in front of, gestured for him to follow. She stopped at an old freight doorway that had a teak entryway fitted into it. Along one side there was a polished brass intercom and five buzzers.

"So what're you, a stockbroker?" he asked, trying for something like normalcy. The lofts down here, he knew, were in the seven figures. She punched a security number into a keypad; the door buzzed itself ajar.

"Not me," she said, "Denny."

Inside it was industrial chic—red-painted girders, iron piping, exposed brick. In one corner of the foyer a Bridgeport miller stood like a sculpture. The elevator was huge, with an old scissors-action door. She took out a key, inserted it, and they rose four or five floors. When the elevator stopped she slung the door back. It opened directly into the loft area.

"Whoa!" he said, stepping inside.

It was almost a parody of postmodern vogue: a Wurlitzer 1015 with its bubble tubes going, de Stijl chairs, a Betty Boop statue, a Bauhaus this, an Art Nouveau that, Mapplethorpe and Stieglitz on the walls—

"What-a-dump!" he said in his Bette Davis voice.

She tossed her clutch on the Empire sofa, took her jacket off. There was a photo of a little girl—maybe two and a half, three years old—on an endtable in a Victorian frame. She picked it up, held it out to him.

He smiled. What did one say about people's kids?

"Cute," he said; then: "Where is she?"

She turned the photograph back to herself, smiled, reached out and touched the girl's face with her fingertips. It was a gesture that strangely recalled her touching Ernie Kovacs on the poster. He turned away, still a little dazzled by the room.

"She wasn't in color," he found himself saying.

She spun around. "What?"

He saw that she thought he'd meant her daughter. "Betty Boop," he said with a gesture toward the waist-high statue of the cartoon character as a cocktail waitress—red high heels, slinky dress, turquoise eyes. "She was strictly black-and-white. Except for some colorization the Japanese did in the seventies. Trying to update her for TV." He made a gesture of dismissal: "Inauthentic. She has to go."

She was looking at the pert statue, the too-big head, the impossibly small waist. "Well, if it comes to that," she said, sending her gaze across the room, "it *all* has to go. I've got seven more months and then I have to sell." And when he didn't understand: "The divorce settlement. It has 'a structured fiduciary withdrawal.' On Denny's part. I can't keep this place without his money."

Something compassionate seemed called for. "Where will you go?"

She shrugged. "I was going to throw myself on his mercy tonight—" she laughed; this was evidently funny—"offer to sign over my share to him, pay the taxes if he'd pay the mortgage. That way, I'd get to stay here and down the road he'd end up owning the place outright, and incidentally feeling better about his moral self. What do you think? He's *got* the money."

He made a "who knows" gesture.

"Right," she said, like the handwriting was on the wall. She reached behind her, picked up a bottle of something, scotch, a couple of Old-fashioned glasses. "Boop-oop-a-doop."

"Still, it's a great place."

"It's *my* place," she said angrily. "I lived here. *Abbie* lived here. It's hard to just erase—" But she caught herself, hung fire, the glasses pinched between her fingers in one hand, the scotch bottle held by the neck in the other. She eyed him, as if making up her mind about something. "Come here," she said after a minute, "I want to show you something."

And she turned, cut through the furniture. He didn't know what else to do except follow.

It was a bedroom she took him into, partitioned off from the loft space and furnished with a matching art deco bedroom set—1930s, Grand Rapids—bronze hardware and rich waterfall veneers cascading to the floor. Along one wall there was a huge window, a flat-screen TV along another, and in the corner an old Kelvinator refrigerator with deco lightning bolts zagging across its door, out of which she got some ice, poured the scotch. He wasn't used to drinking like this, wondered if she was. She pulled the drapes back from the big window, sat on the low sill with her drink between her knees. She fingered the drapery cord like a rosary.

"I watched it all from here," she said simply.

It took him a second to understand. Then he realized the window faced downtown, toward Battery Park: some warehouse rooftops, a few taller buildings, and then open sky where the World Trade Center should have been. He had for an instant a wild thought that Denny had worked there, that he had died and this whole night—phone message, restaurant, apology—was some twisted pantomime she periodically put herself through. But he just as quickly knew that that was wrong, that that couldn't be it.

"You want to hear a story?" she asked. She rattled the ice cubes in her glass, drank.

"Sure."

She took up the drapery cord again. Then she asked him where he'd been that day, a year ago—everybody would always remember where'd they'd been, right?—and when he told her, said how she'd been getting ready to go rollerblading, that she and Abbie had bought a pair of kiddie roller skates the day before—they were for a three-year-old, hardly rolled at all—and that they were going to skate over to Greene Street, stop into D'Angelo's if the breakfast crowd was gone and have an orange juice and a treat. She'd left Abbie practicing happily on the wooden floor in the loft and come back into the bedroom to check the temperature on the TV. It was September, the weather was changing, did they need sweaters? So she'd turned on the TV and there it was. For a second she'd thought it was some disaster flick, changed the channel, changed it again: but it was everywhere, the twin towers engulfed in flame and smoke. She couldn't begin to convey how bizarre it was to open the drapes and see out her bedroom window—like an even bigger television screen—the same sight.

"There were sirens on the TV and then a split-second later the same sirens outside. It was like two things you were used to keeping separate had fused." She looked at the blank TV, then out at the vista of lights and rooftops. "I had the presence of mind to call to Abbie, to tell her that Mommy would be ready in a minute. I didn't want her coming in and seeing that. And then it was like how was I going to prevent her from seeing it? It wasn't just something bad on the TV. It was there, right outside. I remember thinking if the towers fell—I could only imagine them toppling over, not falling in on themselves— would they reach us?"

She was looking out the window, as if gauging the distance to where the towers should have been.

"Which was stupid of course."

He gazed out the window himself—the view was beautiful: the lights, the low-scudding clouds, the rooftops and building facades.

"I couldn't stop myself from watching. I knew I should go see about Abbie, but I couldn't leave the window. After a while I realized she'd stopped roller-skating—there was no more clack-clack on the floor—but the sirens were so noisy, and the TV sound, that I couldn't tell what she was doing. I kept my hand on the remote in case she came in. But she never did."

And she rested her eyes on him. There was in her face a soft appeal, as if she wanted him to forgive her something, understand her. Outside, like a sound effect, a siren had begun to wail.

"Thousands of people were dying," she said simply, staring back into her lap.

The siren moved closer. She let another minute pass, and then went on.

"What she had done was, she had started playing with the drapery cord on one of the loft windows." And she looked at the cord she had been holding in her hand, traced a fingernail along its weave. Then she let it drop, lifted her head and gazed out into the city. "It was the roller skates," she said after another minute had passed. "She must have slipped. Or when the cord got around her neck, not been able to keep on her feet. I don't know. She was only three. When I found her, her legs were sort of splayed out under her. One of her fingers was between the rope and her neck. Like this—" and without turning back to him, she held her own fingers against her neck. In the loft a clock began striking the hour. "What I can't bear," she said, and then waited to get control of herself, "is what she must have thought those last minutes. The panic, the disbelief of why didn't Mommy come." She paused, as if this last was too much. "I can't bear that."

There was, he saw, a tear in her eye—nothing like the breakdown on his message machine—just a wetness that brimmed and threatened to spill over.

"I tried calling 911," she said, and here something of the absurd circumstance of what had happened must have struck her because she let out a horrible laugh. "But of course I couldn't get through—the World Trade Center was collapsing. I didn't know CPR but I tried anyway. Kneeled down on the floor and tried to blow air into her lungs. Oh, I knew she was dead. She had turned blue just like you hear about, and there was no pulse. I carried her down into the street, crying and stumbling and screaming for help, but—" and here again the crazed spurt of laughter escaped her—"the World Trade Center was collapsing. There was no one to help. There were no taxis. Everyone was panicking, running, watching the sky. I found a policeman over on Broadway with his squad car in the middle of the street blocking traffic from going downtown. I tried to get him to help me, but—" and then she said it a third time, as if the horrific coincidence of it, the nightmare collusion, was something she would never get over—"the World Trade Center was collapsing, and what was the death of a little girl to that?"

He could see her in the TV screen, her reflection, and behind her the starbursts of colored lights all the way out to the Battery. She had turned her face to him. But he wasn't looking at her.

"And now I can't bear to leave the loft."

He imagined the men in 1931 Grand Rapids, grateful to have a job still, their younger buddies laid off, the Depression all around like a rainy day. He supposed some of them—one of them anyway—had been in the first world war, had known the mud and the death and the fear. He had touched that furniture, maybe done the varnish job, laying on coat after coat in the quiet of the finishing room, rubbing it out with pumice, then rottenstone.

"You probably noticed all her stuff around."

He hadn't noticed it. But he nodded his head gently.

"And you understand?"

He tried to look kindly.

"What you said about the past. All those postcards and stuff. It's a way to keep it alive, isn't it?"

"Yes," he managed.

"Denny says it's unhealthy. He says a decent interval of mourning has passed. He says having all her things here only makes it worse. But I say—" and she let her voice drop to a lower register—"as long as her things are here, she's here. I can feel her in them. It's like what you said about Charles Atlas and the back pages of comic books. When I see her Play-Doh, or her Tweety-Bird toothbrush, or her tricycle—you noticed it outside, didn't you?—then I see her. When I see her Dorothy doll on the living room floor, it's like she's just stepped out for a minute, gone to the bathroom, or she's getting a change of clothes from the toybox." She let out a laugh, euphoric, a little drunk. "I've kept everything! I've even got her dirty laundry. Her pajamas, her clothes from the day before. They're still unwashed, lying where she left them on the floor of her room. Just wait until she comes home! I'm going to march her in there and tell her to pick them up. Young lady. I'll say that." And she tried it out—"Young lady!"—turning a face to him that managed somehow to be both radiant with belief and horrified. He tried to smile back. But his face was frozen.

"You just march yourself in there, young lady, and pick up your room!"

She stabbed him with her smile. And then, before her face could collapse, she picked up her glass, tossed her head back and drank. But it was no good. Her chin began to quiver, her shoulders began to shake, and then she was lost. A deep, shuddering weeping took hold of her. She turned away from him, sobbed into the window panes.

For the first time that evening he wanted to touch her, to reach out and comfort her. He looked at her stricken form, the thin body convulsed with sobs. He knew he should stand up and cross to her. And then he knew he should leave. And then he had the thought that he would write to her, saw in a lovely, generous, impossible flash an entire future in which he and this woman, even though they would never see one another again, would collude in the making of a world, a world in which Abbie would forever be away at school or camp or college, but like a good girl always writing home, her penmanship changing from year to year, her life kept real with poison ivy, skinned knees, boyfriend troubles . . .

He stood up. She had lifted her feet up onto the sill, was sitting there with her face buried in her knees, hands clasped around her shins. It would be a simple thing for him to go to her, to put his arms around her. And it would be the right thing, wouldn't it? And yet he couldn't do it. He couldn't do it. He looked around the bedroom, at the realness of the furniture, the blankness of the TV screen, watched for a minute the heaving shoulders, and then turned and quietly left the room.

Back in the loft he saw—how had he missed them before?—toys and clothes and coloring books lying haphazardly about the huge space. It was just as she'd said. As if a child had only just left the room, was just outside your vision, your hearing, your ken.

He took the stairs, managed to find—when he realized he needed a key for the elevator—a metal fire door that opened onto a concrete stairwell, and descended floor by floor until he reached the foyer.

Outside, the street was empty and the air was cold. He paused on the sidewalk. How quiet it was! There was the murmur of traffic, but it was distant, away, seemed to sift from the sky downward onto his hair and shoulders. He looked up at the top floor of the building, at the row of lit windows, empty, then let his eyes fall to the tricycle tucked into a doorway off the loading dock. Somewhere, avenues over, a siren sang. He started slowly along the sidewalk, then stopped and listened. It was as if there were something to hear—in the city, in the night—something someone was trying to tell him. He held his breath and waited, stared into the air. But there was only the world, with its intolerable intensity, its unbearable absence.

Moral Problem #6:
PARACONSISTENT LOGIC

You have just finished the chapter in which you disprove the existence of mermaids. Or, as you would prefer to phrase it, the chapter in which you *prove* the *nonexistence* of mermaids. This follows chapters in which you disprove the existence—we beg your pardon—in which you *prove* the *nonexistence* of, in order: the gryphon, the phoenix, and the unicorn. The chapter on mermaids—half-fish, half-human, after all—is a pivotal chapter. It sets the terms for all that will follow. For you will move on, from here, to prove the nonexistence of, first, the platypus, then the penguin, then the fox terrier. Do we catch your drift? You are so excited, you can barely sit still.

It was Averroes who defined logic as "the tool for distinguishing between the true and the false." But it will be you who is remembered as having used logic to prove the nonexistence of the existent. Aristotle did not like the carnival of the excluded middle. Łukasiewicz allowed a new value, the possible, into the tent. You, on the other hand, are simultaneously barker and rube, sideshow freak and ringmaster, cracking your whip at words chasing their own tails.

By the time you get to the chapter that proves the nonexistence of human beings, you and your reader will be sporting in a sea of contradiction and indeterminacy. You have notes for this already. It will be a tour-de-force of paraconsistent logic. It makes you so excited you feel like you are going to pee your pants. You get up from your computer, ruffle your hair, stalk about the house, end up in the kitchen eating a stale cupcake your daughter baked for her birthday a couple of days ago. Which daughter, you can't remember. You have two. It was one or the other.

PUNISHMENT

She told the police she couldn't remember anything. From out of the pain and the dim apprehension that she was alive, shook her head "no." Even after she'd been stabilized and the swelling had gone down so that she could see—though her vision was blurred and the IV-drip made her mind hover just out of reach—still she told them "no." She heard the doctors explain that memory loss was consistent with her injuries: maxillofacial trauma, concussion, hemorrhagic shock. In time, they said, she might remember.

She had not been raped. There was no semen, no vaginal abrasion. But her breasts were horribly bruised, an eggplant purple that made the LPN gasp when she came to give her a bath. Her right eye socket was fractured, her nose too; her jaw was dislocated and three teeth were knocked out; one of her lips had to be sewed back together. Her whole face was blue and yellow and purple. Her face and her breasts—there were no other injuries.

She made it known that she did not want anyone to see her like this. That Emily should stay with her father. That she didn't want to see Bill, or her mother, or the press. No one. When they moved her out of the ICU, Bill phoned but it wasn't easy for her to speak, so he did the talking, let her know that Emily was all right, but that the police had been by to question him. "The ex-husband," he'd said and there it was, even over the phone, even now. Did she remember anything yet? he asked. She found herself shaking her head "no," and again: "no," and then in a strangled voice saying the words into the phone: "no, I'm sorry, nothing."

———

But she did remember. She remembered everything. She remembered the man, his face, his voice. She remembered his wrist watch, and his tie, and the wedding ring on the wrong finger. She remembered trying to protect her face, and how he had pummeled her breasts, and when she tried to protect her breasts, how he had beaten her face. And she remembered going in and out of consciousness. And choking on her own blood. And she remembered thinking she was going to die.

She had driven out to the Arboretum that day to cleanse herself of the bitter wives and the injured husbands she'd spent the morning with in her courtroom. She had parked in her usual spot, in the turnaround down along the highway, changed into her Reeboks and started up through the gentle path toward the monastery. It was early April and the last of the snow melt ran in braids underfoot. As she climbed she heard, over the tops of the trees, the lovely sound of the chapel bells ringing the hour.

She didn't see him at first. And then she did. He was keeping pace with her, coming down alongside her on a fork that led up to the cloister gate. For a second she thought it might be one of the nuns—she caught flashes of black between the trees—but no, it was a man in a suit. Just like her, dressed all wrong for a walk in the woods. When their paths came together she slowed down, tried to let him go on ahead, but instead he matched his step to hers and said "hello." He was handsome, clean-shaven, with that forced tan that a certain kind of handsome man maintains. There was a diamond stud in his right earlobe. "Smart," he said with a glance down at her Reeboks and then a rueful look at his own muddy loafers. So she smiled at him. And then he hit her.

She didn't scream. She was too stunned for that, sitting there on her fanny in the mud—stupidly, grotesquely. Her nose felt like it had exploded. "What?" she managed to say. As if she were asking for clarification. And then he was astraddle her, punching her over and over again, and it was too late to scream.

So this was it, she remembered thinking. This was how it was going to happen. She'd always imagined it in a dank parking garage, or coming home to a dark house—imagined it so many times that it took her a moment to realize she wasn't being raped. He was not raping her. This was something else.

He got tired once or twice and had to stop to rest. These were the times she came back to consciousness.

———

Toward the end of her hospital stay a police detective came by with a plastic briefcase of photographs for her to look at. They were photos of all the men in the cases she had adjudicated in the last year. She marveled at the work it must have involved, tracking down the ex-wives, talking them out of old wedding photos, photos of the bowling team. She recognized the men, recalled their quavering voices, their sheepishness, their moments of anger, of injury.

"No," she told the detective, shaking her head at each photo. "No, I'm sorry."

When she was released the doctors warned her to be on the lookout for worsening headaches, for numbness, slurred speech. If she experienced problems with reasoning, they wanted her to call them. Also if she had any further difficulty with memory. On the other hand she should expect mood swings, lapses in coordination and balance, but if these worsened, they wanted to see her. They would assess her in another week when the shield on her nose would need to be removed. And of course, her stitches. In the meantime they would put her in touch with a maxillofacial surgeon.

When she got home there were eleven days of the *Hartford Courant* waiting for her on her porch. She was front page news—*Superior Court Judge Brutally Assaulted*—with a photo of her in her robe, and a photo of the path in the Arboretum. "Left for dead," the paper said.

She called her mother in Flagstaff. She called Bill.

"I'm going to be as good as new," she said with a smile in her voice while Emily sobbed into the phone. She was still her princess! Her bug! But she'd have to stay with her father a little longer. Just until her mom got better. And when Bill came back on: "Is she okay? Has there been any change?"

"She won't let me look at her," Bill said.

"Her wrists? Her arms?"

"She's wearing these long-sleeve things."

———

She didn't know what to do with herself. She formalized her leave, fended off friends, colleagues, the press. She watched the National Spelling Bee on afternoon ESPN, picked up a needlepoint kit she'd abandoned years ago. She cleaned the grout on the bathroom tile.

When the house became too oppressive she tried the movies. But she was afraid she'd meet someone she knew, so more often she found herself just going for drives, in and around Hartford, out past the Indian casinos, down along the Sound. She got gas at the full-service pumps so she didn't have to get out of the car, meals at the Drive-Thrus. At Hammonasset she took her shoes off and walked along the edge of the frigid surf. The sandpipers ran panicked ahead of her.

She tried to talk to Emily as often as Emily would let her, confined herself to innocent topics—what were they playing in Band? did she need new clothes? Emily answered in single words, half-sentences. The mother heard her own voice—half-hysterical it seemed, trying to sound so chipper—saying how when this was all over they would rent that place on the

Vineyard again, just the two of them lying in the sun facing France: didn't that sound good?

She found herself from time to time driving past her old grade school. She was not the sentimental type but the sight of the girls in the playground with their plaid skirts and white blouses, the sky-blue niche over the main entrance with its Virgin Mary, drew her in some obscure way. Inside she walked through the familiar hallways and tried to feel nostalgic. A hall monitor—she had been one herself in the sixth grade—looked up from her metal desk, her yellow pencil with its pink eraser suspended in wonder. Everything she looked at—the green bulletin board, the waxed floor, the chipped black paint that spelled "GIRLS" on the lavatory door—everything was familiar and yet strangely off. She felt a little taken aback. It hadn't been so long, after all, just two years since she'd returned to accept the school's Prudence Crandall Award—"Local girl makes adequate," she had taken to saying at cocktail parties. But now she felt simultaneously part of the past and remote from it, as if she expected any instant a classroom door to open and Roberta Rossi and Donna Szotek to come filing out in their uniforms, looking up in momentary wonder at the adult woman with the scarred, mealy face.

When she was ten she had taken a vow to live without doing anything wrong. *Without doing anything wrong!* It had only lasted a month or so, but for that month she had tried—not just to follow the rules: she had always followed the rules—but to not be mean, or selfish, or stuck-up. Because the world was God's. Everything in it was God's. Everything was directed and purposeful, and so anything dirty or mean was God's punishment of someone for something. Bobby Hines and his harelip, Tony Costa's spittle when he declared to everyone that you *went down*—they were all instruments of God, His ugly angels telling you something, something you needed to know.

"What?" she whispered now—standing there in the hallway with the ghost of her childhood around her—what was it that she needed to know?

———

The Saturday after she was fitted with a bridge she made a date with Emily. It was her grief counselor's idea. It was also his idea that Emily not move back right away, that she needed time to get used to what had happened. When she told Emily this over the phone Emily said that that was okay, she didn't want to move back anyway. She liked it at her dad's.

"We'll go somewhere, somewhere neutral," the mother said in a calm voice.

"Nothing's neutral."

"Like the mall," she suggested. "This grief counselor suggested the mall."

"Terry Gulko felt me up and then broke up with me at the mall."

"No, he didn't."

"Nothing's neutral."

At first her daughter wouldn't look at her, climbing into the car with her hair hanging on either side of her face, staring out through the windshield and complaining about her pantyhose. But as they drove, the mother could feel the daughter's gaze resting on the side of her face. It was her bad side, the side with the drooping eyelid, the red cicatrix from the stitches, but she let Emily look, kept up a chatter about this and that, finally, desperately, about plastic surgery and how maybe she'd get a whole new face, a movie star face. She'd be the Hepburn of the Connecticut Superior Court, what did Emily think?

"Audrey?" Emily muttered into her hair. "Or Katherine?"

In the mall they went from store to store, holding up skirts and blouses to one another. It was almost normal. They bought Emily some culottes, a cashmere pullover, some size 8's for her slimmed-down Mom. In Waldenbooks Emily went to browse in the Fantasy section while her mother roamed distracted—things were going okay, weren't they?—through Fiction, Computing, Self-Help. She picked up a book on No-Fault *Divorce*, thumbed through the platitudes and evasions. It made her want to scream. What did she see from the bench every day except that everyone was at fault? Everyone was wrong, selfish, vengeful, spiteful, blind. It was all she could do sometimes to follow the guidelines of Family Court and not slam her gavel down and start handing out prison sentences: two years at Montville for loss of affection, twenty years for adultery leading to a scared child—

In a retro ice-cream parlor with their shopping bags spilled around them, Emily asked out of nowhere if it still hurt.

And so she told her about it. Not about the attack itself but about the doctors and the pain medication, the muscle relaxants, and about her room not having a mirror in it, and her mandible immobilized so she had to eat through a straw, about the upcoming surgery and how she hadn't wanted to go to this grief counselor the hospital had referred her to but now she was glad she had, because he was so helpful—

"All in all it's not the worst thing that's happened to me," she wound up with what was supposed to be a rueful smile, and then to cover herself began to tell about this game she'd played in college where you had to say what the worst thing that had ever happened to you was and then what the worst thing you'd ever *done* was, and how it was strange that everybody admitted to *gross* things they'd done, but no one would say what the, you know, *worst* thing was.

"And what's the worst thing *you* ever did, Judge?"

"Oh," she sang, smiling, searching in the distance for the answer. She had always been Little Miss Perfect, had never had to write I *will not talk in class* one hundred times. Had never smashed pumpkins, never gotten a speeding ticket. In college she'd owned up to eating chocolate-covered ants in Mexico not because she was deflecting the moral with the gross, but because she'd been embarrassed at how piddling her real trans-gressions were.

"Falling out of love with your father," she found herself an-swering. Emily rolled her eyes like, *sure*. The mother slurped her milkshake so things wouldn't get too heavy.

"You wanna know what the *best* thing I ever did is?" she asked after a minute.

"No."

"You wanna know?"

"No."

"Giving birth to you. *That's* the best thing I ever did."

The best thing! she wanted to scream as Emily grimaced, stood up, busied herself with her shopping bags.

And was that why she was cutting herself with knives, with X-acto blades, sitting on the edge of her bed and, in what the mother imagined was a kind of hypnosis, slicing away at her body, her being, her Emily-ness?

———

She remembered the flash of the diamond stud in his earlobe.

She remembered the wedding ring on the wrong finger.

And she remembered, coming back to consciousness once, hearing him speaking in a panting, ecstatic voice.

You know what this is for! he was saying, hitting her. *You know what this is for!*

———

At the clinic she showed the plastic surgeon photos of her old nose. He answered with silhouettes of noses on his computer. She tried to turn his attention back to her photos, but it was the silhouettes—morphing almost imperceptibly on the screen—that he would use as his reference. She had the strange sense—sitting there with pictures of her young self sprawled on her lap—the strange sense that her nose was leaving her. It made her laugh out loud. The doctor looked surprised. She apolo-gized, then laughed again, tried to describe to him her nose walking out the door with its suitcases, but she was laughing too much, choking even, and then—oh, good Lord!—she was sobbing, sobbing out loud uncontrollably.

"Sorry," she gasped. "Sorry."

The doctor smiled nervously, held out a tissue.

"What's that movie—?" she managed to say after a minute in between hiccups. She was bending over, trying to pick up her photos from where they'd spilled onto the floor. "That movie where these aliens come and—" she had to sit up, had to catch her breath; the surgeon looked scared—"and they take away people's bodies and leave a, you know, a replica in its place? What's that movie?"

"What?" the surgeon said. He had braces on his teeth. Funny thing for a plastic surgeon to have. "I'm sorry, what?"

———

On the phone Emily said she was serious about not moving back.

"I mean you're going to be dating and everything, right?" she said. "I mean I don't want to get in your way."

"I'm not going to be dating, sweetie . . . "

"I like it here."

Dating? she wanted to scream. Who was going to date her? She was forty-two years old, her face looked like a volcano, her breasts were dying of fat necrosis . . .

"I miss you," she said instead. She kept her voice steady. "I wish you'd move back home." And then—was this unfair? manipulative? was this the worst thing she had ever done?—"It might help me."

"What about what your grief counselor says?"

"He just wanted you to have time to get used to what's happened."

"Maybe you could date him."

"Emily—"

"I don't even know what's happened!" And she hung up.

It was *Invasion of the Body Snatchers*, she muttered, going eighty along the interstate, daring the State troopers. What kind of a plastic surgeon didn't know *Invasion of the Body Snatchers?*

———

What she hated was the way they described her daughter, the picture they drew of some composite cutter: aggressive, hyper-sensitive, attention-seeking, self-hating. That was not her Emily, not her bug!

She had found the site a year ago when the school nurse had called and she had needed to understand this sudden, horrible thing she was being told. She had gotten out onto the web and read everything she could find: case studies, profiles, analyses, treatment, had subscribed to the self-injury newsgroup. But when she had tried to talk to Emily, had taken her to McDonald's armed with what she hoped was understanding, Emily wouldn't even admit anything was wrong. No, she wouldn't go to a doctor. No, it was her mother who should see a therapist. "Come on, bug," she had tried to smile, but at the sound of the childhood endearment Emily's face had gone rigid. They had finished eating in silence. Back at the house she had written down the self-injury website's address and left it for Emily to find. It was all she could think to do.

She had taken, in those days, to lurking in the chat room, listening to the scary discussion, the half-articulate confessions—oh, the things these girls revealed! Every night she had logged on, followed the discussion, wondering where in all this sick horror her Emily was? She tried to understand the diseased logic of it all, the dark compulsion, but she couldn't get past the idea that at its heart—and maybe this was just her, the judge she'd become—at its heart was some need for punishment.

<those teeth things, *hesterprynne* was saying, you know, on scotch tape dispensers>

It made her sick to listen to them, and yet she had to know.

Beneath the veil of hair, behind the averted eyes and the sarcasm and what the mother had thought was self-deprecating wit—was Emily one of these girls? She had never been a happy child. The mother had to admit that. And yet she and Bill had loved her, hadn't they? That first year they had been a team, a real team, spelling one another with their sleepless baby, taking turns bundling her up and wheeling her all over West Hartford in the jogging stroller. There had been one night—she hadn't thought of this in years—one snowy, winter midnight when she had stopped outside Trinity Church and watched the snow falling softly in the streetlight, and then had lifted Emily out of the stroller to show her the crèche—the lambs and oxen and the glinting jewels in the wise men's crowns. She was not given to extravagant gestures and so what had possessed her to do what she did next she didn't know, but she had taken the terracotta Jesus out of his manger, laid him aside, and in the cold, whispering stillness, had put her own baby in his place. Even at the time she'd known it was a bit over the top. But it was also a thing that came out of the deepest place inside her. She couldn't explain it.

Was there no way, she wondered, sitting there in front of her computer half-reading the sick talk, was there no way to tell Emily about that? No way to convince her by the sheer weight of her mother's love to stop? For a moment she trembled with the thought that she might yet make her see. But it only lasted a moment. It wasn't just a question of giving love, was it? Emily had always had love. And still she had shrunk into anger, had moved into such a bizarre world of pain and injury that the mother didn't know how to follow her. And her mother's love—it had the look now of something ill-fitting, didn't it? Like a half-forgotten sundress come across in the attic on a winter day's rummage. What to do with the pretty, useless thing?

<but not knives, *hesterprynne* was saying, too much blood for too little pain>

Her grief counselor asked if she was angry. She said no, she was not angry. Not in the ordinary way.

"Not angry that this bad thing happened to you?"

"It wasn't personal," she found herself saying. "I would be angry if it were personal."

They were sitting in his office with its two clocks, one facing her, the other facing him. He was a small, fit man, a tri-athlete judging by the photos on the wall: him and his 4% body fat in a wet suit; astraddle a racing bike; marathoning through the Arboretum with PUMA plastered across his chest.

"You mean because he didn't know you. It could've been anyone. You were just unlucky."

"Just unlucky," she repeated.

She supposed this was what they called passive-aggressive: her sitting there with her legs crossed, smiling and refusing to acknowledge that she was angry. But he wouldn't under-stand—secular, assured, sorting humanity into Myers-Briggs types—he wouldn't understand how she chose to think of it, that there was a transgression involved—a transgression she didn't understand, but ought to understand.

She smiled at him. He had his fingertips pressed together so that his hands made a little steeple. Their time was almost up.

"I'm your grief counselor," he said. "But you don't seem to be grieving."

———

She parked outside the middle school, kept one eye on the front entrance, one eye on Emily's bus. When the doors opened and the kids began to file out the mother was struck by how misshapen they looked in their sloppy clothes and huge back-packs. Even Emily when she came through the door, hipless, breastless, carrying her skinny flute case. Her hair looked like it hadn't been washed in months. The mother watched in silence as she came down the walk, and then buzzed the passenger-side window down.

"Emily."

The girl looked up as if stung. Then, instead of crossing to where her mother's car sat idling, she flung her eyes down and walked on past. The mother put the car in gear, let it track alongside the curb.

"Hey," she said after a minute through the open window. The girl shifted her flute case from one hand to the other and kept walking. "Jeez, bug. Give me a break."

She stopped and turned to where her mother was leaning over the passenger-side seat, steering the car precariously with her left hand. "What do you want?"

"I just want to talk. I want to show you something."

The girl eyed her furiously. "And then you'll take me where I want? You'll take me to Dad's?"

"If that's what you want."

The daughter waited a theatrical minute, then unslung her backpack, crossed the grassy strip to the curb and slid into the car.

"Okay," she said, "but no funny stuff."

Funny stuff? the mother wondered. "Funny stuff?" she said aloud, trying to strike an old note.

"Just drive."

So she drove, pulled away from the curb, maneuvered through the suburban streets until she got onto the road heading out of town. Emily turned the radio on, turned it off, watched the countryside go by.

"So what did you want to show me?"

She hadn't wanted to show her anything, but now she had to come up with something. "I thought we'd go for a walk."

"I was *going* for a walk. *Judge.*"

"I thought we'd go for a walk in the Arboretum."

She could feel Emily turn her eyes on her, but the girl didn't say anything.

"My grief counselor says it's something I need to do," she

extemporized. She expected some sarcasm over the melodrama, some *oof!* or *oy!* but all she heard was a quiet "okay."

Twenty minutes later they were climbing the path that led toward the monastery. They'd parked the car in the same turnaround she'd used two months ago, a pair of birders there now folding up their spotting scope, and at the other end of the turnaround a Lexus SUV that made her pause a moment: it was so exactly what *he* would drive. They walked a little apart, using the roots for footholds until the path began to level out. There was a piney smell in the undergrowth. The ground was dry. The air was warm. It felt different from that day.

When they reached the spot she had the urge to just keep going. She would tell Emily about it later. But even as she was thinking this, she stopped. Emily walked on a few steps and then turned back with a questioning look. The place was so innocent-looking: the two paths converging, the ground matted with leaves, a grove of ferns off to the side where the sun broke through the canopy. The mother had nearly died here. Why?

Emily was doing that thing she did sometimes, pulling on her cuffs so they covered the heels of her hands. A cicada's whine split the heavy air.

What, the mother wondered, had she expected? There was nothing here. There was nothing in the dead leaves, in the gentle path leading upward to the monastery, nothing in the light filtering through the leaves overhead that wanted to reveal itself.

"It could've been someplace else," she said. She looked off to the side, to where she had fallen into the mud when he'd hit her.

"And you still don't remember anything?" Emily asked.

She could see the outline of the mud puddle. Dried out now, but the red earth with a residual sheen. Some little evidence anyway.

"No," she answered. "Nothing."

She started walking again, not up the path she had been climbing that day, but up the one that led to the monastery, the one he had been coming down.

"Mom."

She turned back to where Emily was still standing. There was a look struggling across her face, as if the girl didn't want the moment to pass unmarked, but didn't know what to say or how to say it. The mother smiled at her, held out her hand.

"Come on, bug," she said. "There's nothing here."

So they kept on, up through the woods into some birches and then along the stone wall that marked off the cloistered part of the arboretum. It was more open here, with clumps of mountain laurel and blueberry bushes. As they walked they could feel the sun's heat radiating from the stone wall. Up ahead the chapel belltower loomed through the trees.

"Do you believe in God?" the mother found herself calling back to her daughter.

"What?" she heard behind her, then: "No. Do you?"

She shook her head "no".

A few minutes later they turned through the stone gate into the monastery yard. There was a standpipe the mother knew about; they would have a drink, and then start back. It was quiet in the yard, the buildings dark and serene with their narrow leaded windows, their stone lintels and copper roofs. Along the driveway two nuns were kneeling in a flowerbed. A John Deere four-wheeler was parked alongside them on the lawn. Emily made a face and nodded silently toward them, as if she'd spotted some wildlife she didn't want to spook. They walked past without speaking. The green lawn stretched to the woods' edge. There was only the sound of their feet on the drive, and the scrape of the nuns' trowels. They drew up to where a galvanized pipe peeked from between some laurel, turned the spigot on and drank.

"Boy, it's hot," Emily whispered.

They were both perspiring from the walk. They drank again,

wiped their lips with the backs of their hands. Emily couldn't help but look over her mother's shoulder back at the nuns.

"What do they do all day?" she whispered.

"Work," the mother answered. She turned and looked back along the arcing drive at the two figures in their scapulars, their bodies bent over their gardening. "And pray. They keep bees. And there's a gift shop."

The mother watched her daughter look, ran her eyes over the wondering face. How perfect her skin was! And her green eyes with those mustard-colored flecks! And the little scar along her jaw where she'd been hit with a rake when she was five and had to go to the emergency room.

"Weird," Emily said. She was still looking at the nuns. Above them, the chapel began ringing the half-hour.

"You want to go inside?" the mother asked.

"What?"

"The chapel," she said, and gestured with her head. "It'll be cool."

The girl shrugged. "I don't care."

So she led her across the lawn, up the paved walk. They stood for a moment on the granite stoop, listening to the summer silence, the heat and the insects. And then Emily reached for the iron latch. One of the nuns looked up at the sound of the heavy door swinging open.

Inside, they had to remain standing at the rear of the little nave until their eyes got used to the light. Off to the left was a doorway that led darkly to the nuns' quarters. And ahead of them the altar, the stations of the cross along the walls. When they started down the aisle the mother found herself genuflecting.

"Wow," Emily whispered, looking around at the gothic dark.

They slipped into a pew, and the mother—again, how the old habit survived!—slid down onto the wooden kneeler.

Emily, at a loss, knelt beside her, put her hands together on the pew in front of her and rested her forehead on her thumbs.

"What're we doing?" she whispered after a minute.

"Praying," the mother answered.

Another minute passed. And then the girl turned her head and whispered toward her mother, "I don't know how. What do you say?"

The mother peered into the darkness under the pew. What had she used to say, when she was a girl? And where had all those prayers gone, hers and her schoolmates', lifting like a flock of birds into the air? From outside came the sound of the four-wheeler starting up. It idled for a minute, and then moved off, down the drive, away.

"I've been lying," she heard herself say. She closed her eyes and inhaled the damp, stony air.

"What?" came the voice beside her. The word was barely a whisper.

"The attack," the mother said. "I remember it. I remember everything."

And she turned her head so she could see Emily's face. It was tilted on its side, so some of her hair fell across her eye.

"Why?" the girl asked.

She thought a moment, looked over Emily's shoulder to the wall where the stained glass windows scattered colored light across the pews. "It was a way of—" of what? what exactly?— "of accepting punishment."

The word seemed to bruise the air between them. "Punishment?" Emily repeated. They were still kneeling, the sides of their heads resting on their hands. Some intelligence, some understanding seemed to tremble between them. And then Emily was turning her head away, laying her other cheek upon her crossed hands so that the back of her head was to her mother. "What did you need to be punished for?" the mother heard a small voice ask.

"For everything," she answered. For her marriage gone wrong, she wanted to say, for the way her love of the law had died in her courtroom. "For everything," she whispered again, and then, barely audible: "For not being able to save you."

No, she had never been any good at praying. Her prayers had always been hopelessly grandiose or selfish—that the famine in Bangladesh would end, that she'd get her period like Donna Szotek had. A *good* girl, a valedictorian, later on a volunteer at the Women's Center—still, she had made a mess of it.

"I don't need to be saved."

She looked at the back of Emily's head, at the ripple of her backbone inside her blouse. Her daughter, her thirteen-year-old daughter.

"We all need to be saved," she said. And saying it, she felt in her heart the old urge to comfort, the old delicious urge to hold Emily and tell her everything was all right—she was her perfect baby, her perfect bug! But at the sight of the pained face turning to her, the old comforts fell away. She reached out, and for the first time in months touched her daughter, let her fingers rest lightly on Emily's forearm.

"Let me see them," she said.

The girl's eyes quickened. She lifted herself from off the kneeler, sat back in the pew. The mother sat back too.

"What?"

So she tried again, this time without touching her. "Let me see them."

The girl set her body defiantly, scraped the hair back from her face. And then she was doing it, pulling her sleeve up over her elbow, first her right arm, then her left. She held them out for her mother to see. There, up and down each forearm, on the pale underside where there was no hair, was a column of scars—pinkish, tender still, but on their way to healing.

"You've stopped," the mother murmured. She looked from the scars to the girl's face. "Emily!"

Above them, the belltower began ringing the three-quarters hour. The sound seeped through the stone walls, spread through the darkness under their pew. Emily waited until it had drained away, and then without taking her eyes off her mother's face, reached down and pulled her blouse out of her pants so her stomach was exposed.

It was like a scream carved into her abdomen. The mother let out a cry, looked up to Emily's trembling eyes and then back down to the pale skin with its horrible red blaze. She covered her mouth with her hand, stared at the wound. It seemed almost readable, like a hieroglyph. "Dear God," she whispered. She reached out and with the tips of her fingers felt the soft swell of her daughter's belly, the raised rib of the scabs. She held her breath. Somewhere in the cloister a door was opening.

"Emily," she whispered.

She felt herself begin to swoon. There were footsteps approaching from somewhere. The air darkened.

"You know what this is for," she heard a voice saying. The girl's flesh quaked under her fingertips. "*You know what this is for.*"

Moral Problem #7:
THE PIGEONS AT KAZAN CATHEDRAL

No one asks anymore except the ghosts, but if they did, this is what you would say:

You would say that the letter was written by you and by no one else. That you yourself posted it to *Leningradskaya Pravda*. That you were not and had never been approached by anyone from the Union of Soviet Writers or the secret police. That Comrade Akhmatova's subsequent expulsion from the writers' union and the arrest and imprisonment of her son had nothing to do with you. You wrote the letter because your husband died in the war and your baby died during the siege and because you saw her when she returned after the blockade and the sight of her alongside the Fontanka Canal—well-fed, celebrated, alive—angered you.

It was summer then. Your knees were still bulbous from the famine, your arms like wands, but you were feeling so much better that you managed to walk the kilometer to the Hall of Columns where you heard some of her poetry read. And there was that one poem about her Leningrad and the war suffering and the pigeons in front of Kazan Cathedral and that is what you attacked her for. Because there had been no pigeons in front of Kazan Cathedral during the siege, no pigeons there or anywhere else in Leningrad. They had all been eaten. The pigeons and the crows, the dogs and the cats. You had been there. You had seen it. You had boiled your handbag into jelly, fed your baby the horsehide

119

paste from off the back of your bedroom wallpaper. Comrade Akhmatova had not.

So you wrote your letter and it became part of the uproar, evidence of the famous poet's enmity to the Soviet order, her *antinarodnost*. And people knew who you were. They pointed you out. The braver ones asked you about it.

That was sixty years ago. Now in front of the Winter Palace half-naked teenagers eat out of McDonald's bags and listen to Run-DMC. BMWs fly past the Admiralty. You walk through the tangerine- and lemon-colored city in a kind of delirium, talking to the statues, to the ghosts, to the mounded earth in the Piskariovskoye Cemetery. The tourists wonder at you, but they have come to see St. Petersburg and you, you live in Leningrad.

In the winter you can still see them, the corpses on the street corners. They are wrapped in sheets or someone's parlor curtains. Up and down Nevsky Prospekt the trolley cars sit shagged in ice. There is no electricity to run them. No way to clear the tracks of snow. Inside—did they stop to rest and never get up again?— there are corpses seated, facing forward, waiting. They will still be there tomorrow when you pass, and the next day.

In Hay Square you can tell the ones who have given in. They have hot eyes and pink cheeks. They sell packets of ground meat for rubles, for jewelry, for your wedding ring. If you ask them, they will tell you it is horsemeat. You cross yourself at the sight of them, step into the street to go around them. A car honks at you but of course there are no cars. There is no petrol. You make your way through the snowdrifts. There is the impossible smell of American french fries. Somewhere a businesswoman is talking on a cell phone. When finally you reach the cemetery the corpses are stacked like railroad sleepers.

When you saw her, years later, standing in the market along the Obvodny Canal in a shawl and a karakul coat, sorting through a vendor's boots—how worn her own were!—should you have gone up to her? Should you have gone up to her and explained who you were, asked her for forgiveness?

On Sadovaya Street you walk behind a child's sled being pulled by two skeletons. Draped across the sled is a woman with frozen skin. She stares up at the winter sky. She has no coat on. Her hair trails behind her in the snow.

Back at your flat you lie on your bed. In the next room your nine-month-old daughter lies in a laundry basket. She has been dead for six days. For six days you have not had the strength to get out of bed and carry her across the city to the stack of dead outside the cemetery. The wallpaper is gone from the walls of your room. Out your window a foot is sticking out of the ice in the Obvodny Canal. In a moment, you tell yourself, you will get up. In a moment you will have the strength and you will get up and go out into the city. You will walk to the cemetery. You will do that, at least, for her.

DESTROYING HERMAN YODER

In the gun store I couldn't make up my mind. There was all that smug menace to choose from. I hefted revolvers and breech loaders, practiced executing the world with Mausers and Glocks. The store owner—his name was Ronnie—was very patient, answering my questions, overlooking my ignorance. In the end it was a Smith & Wesson snub-nosed .38 Special I settled on, swayed I suppose by the associations—fedoras, rain-slick alleys, platinum blondes and gut-shot punks. I have always been a classicist at heart, as even the Academy of American Poets recognized.

According to *The Review of Wound Ballistics*, the Glaser Safety Slug (one of which I have just discharged into a pumpkin to the right of Herman Yoder's head) has a pre-fragmented core of compressed number twelve shot. It uses an eighty grain bullet rated at +P velocity, a design that causes the slug to expend its energy into the target, without excessive penetration and the danger of collateral injury.

I say all this to Herman Yoder, standing there in his living room, even that part about the +P velocity, smiling calmly the way madmen do in the movies.

It was not easy finding him. Yoder is a common surname in Iowa. Drive through the environs of the Amana colonies and you will see it painted sloppily on every other mailbox. I had to thumb though a dozen phone books, call this or that Yoder and impersonate lost high-school buddies, confused delivery men, until finally I located his house in a cornfield outside Wellman, just down the road from a wooden church on the National Historic Register, a mere eighteen miles from the high school he'd attended, twenty-two from the farm Grace Albrecht had grown up on.

"What kind of name is that anyway?" I say now, coming back from the pumpkin and plopping myself down in this sad Castro convertible. I keep the gun leveled at him.

"Yoder," he says, as if that explained something.

"Not Yoder," I say; and then like a punch line: "Herman. What kind of dick-ass name is that?"

The Review of Wound Ballistics. Don't you love it?

The Castro convertible isn't the only sad thing here. The whole house is sad in my considered opinion. A suburban rambler, circa 1970, an out-of-place eyesore with its pseudo-modernist horizontals, low-pitched roof, the nonsense of a lawn abutting cornfield on three sides. There's a little windmill in the front yard. Maybe five feet tall. And in the backyard a split-log yard swing. Very rustic.

Somewhere, acres away, a harvester is running. Rolled up in my back pocket I've got my well-thumbed copy of *Action Comics #187.*

He asks for the second time who I am, and for the second time I tell him. I am Ichabod Sick, I say, which is more or less true.

"What kind of name is that?" he has the nerve to say and I smile, make a checkmark in the air to show I appreciate the bravado.

"Sick," I say and cock the Special. "That's what kind of name."

Twenty years ago it had been a choice between Ichabod and Orlando, dactyl or amphibrach. I took a poll of friends and enemies. Orlando, it was felt, had a certain flair which, in my warmer moments toward myself, appealed—thick, Harlequin-Romance hair, a chemise open at the throat, maybe a casement window dusted with Tuscan moonlight. Or so I described it years later to an interviewer from *The American Poetry Review*. But Ichabod had a doggy tenacity that I thought would stick by me when the going got tough. When I handed the official papers in, the Cambridge District Court secretary had grimaced.

"Sid Vicious," she'd said. This was 1981. "Johnny Rotten. Is that the idea?"

Herman Yoder, on the other hand, looks like a Nashville reject. A blonde-streaked mullet that's already getting on my nerves, a ripped "Achy-Breaky" T-shirt, blue jeans. I caught him barefooted and about to shave, which gives him a particularly vulnerable air. It's a pleasure to find him so easy to hate.

I tell him to sit on his hands. To put his hands under his thighs and keep them there. This was something my high school chess coach taught the chess team to do. "Think," he used to say. "Then think some more. Don't take your hands out until you understand the position on the board."

"Think," I tell Herman Yoder now. "Then think some more. Don't take your hands out until you understand the position on the board."

He wants to know what he's supposed to think about.

"Crime and punishment," I tell him.

In addition to Herman Yoder, and Ichabod Sick, and the pumpkin with a bullet in its brain, the other sad entities in Herman Yoder's living room are a television, a couch, photos of what one surmises is Herman Yoder's family. Tucked in between two chairs there's a bookcase filled with diet books. Taped on the picture window, facing out, made of construction paper, are two black cats, a witch on a broomstick, and an impossibly orange moon.

On the end table beside me is the 1990 Clear Creek Amana High School yearbook (faux-leather binding, faux-gilt lettering). I open it at the back and start paging through it. There's a Zelinsky, and a Zeiner. And then there's a Yoder. Three Yoders actually—Anna, Eva, and Herman. We ask the Herman in the photo if he knows that he will grow up to wear an Achy-Breaky T-shirt like a capital-L loser, and then flip to the front of the book.

Aaron, Abbott, Adamczyk,—you should quit now, we tell ourselves, but the pages keep turning—Adamson, Ahling, Aiken . . .

And then there she is, her eighteen-year-old self, looking at me from off the page without reproach or shadow, in one of her cape dresses, and with a prayer veil covering her hair, and with that smile of hers, and for a moment the world shimmers again, coheres, and the urge to kill living things that has been hovering just above the Castro convertible drifts toward the open window—

———

The first time I saw her I was twenty-five and she was twelve. I was a hotshot in the Iowa Writers' Workshop, the lithium/valproate cocktail that had gotten me through college was still working, and I was living with a girl who liked to expose her breasts to me as if they were a force of nature. Her name was Judith, and she was ironic and Jewish and thought Iowa was a hoot.

It was at the Steam Days Celebration in Kalona, where Judith and I had gone because that's what we did on weekends, attended rural Iowa as if it were a local talent show. There were restored tractors and harvesters on display, steam-powered antiquities with belts flapping and pop valves hissing. A bingo game was being called over a PA system. We walked around and made fun of everything, ate bratwurst and roasted corn, rubbed sunscreen on each other's bare limbs. Judith had on these big sunglasses that made her look like Jackie O. And I had on a tank top because in those days I was lean and had nice arms. We turned into the main tent where pies and fresh-baked bread and handicrafts were being sold. It was Judith who spotted her.

I captured the moment beautifully in "The Atmosphere Cleaves." That sense of another world intruding on this one.

A higher world depositing here as a joke or a parable—or just to rub our noses in our lame, drooling, mud-caked, manic-depressive inadequacy—a splash of clarity. She was with her mother, standing behind a card table with a checked table-cloth flung over it, selling jars of homemade preserves and jellies, the two of them in Mennonite dress, their hair parted in the middle and swept back under a little cap, their bodies in unflattering, homemade dresses that covered their arms and dropped to their ankles, identical Reeboks on their feet. This was nothing to me. I had gotten used to seeing Menno-nite families on shopping excursions in the malls around Iowa City. But there was about this girl a lucid beauty that was un-nerving. Not Hollywood or *Vogue* beauty, understand. There were no flaring cheekbones. She had only as much mouth as was necessary. But her face was perfect. A beauty as bare of ornament as an equation.

"We must have intercourse," Judith said, parting the red slash of her lips and poking me in the ribs. "We must sample her wares."

What I remember most, and what made it into "The Atmo-sphere Cleaves," was the sudden sense of my own carnality, the nakedness of my limbs, my shoulders, the bare crankshafts of Judith's collarbones. I saw myself, saw Judith and me, as this girl must have seen us—in our vanity, our sex unredeemed by any glimmer of love. Judith did all the talking, sampling the various jellies and preserves—plum, peach, apple but-ter—commenting on each and asking questions. Each time it was the mother who responded, even when Judith directed her questions at the girl, who stood there shy and overwhelmed. The only word she uttered was "Grace" when Judith—from point-blank range—asked her her name.

"Grace," Judith repeated, and the word slithered in the air and disappeared into the undergrowth. "And how old are you, Grace?"

"She's twelve," the mother said, handing me the change. She noticed my hand tremors. The lithium.

"And do you say your prayers every night?"

A glaze overspread mother and daughter. They were used to this. The sly harassment, the indirect ridicule.

"Come on," I said, taking Judith by the arm. She smiled her Scarsdale-Vassar, we-have-to-be-going smile, and let me lead her away.

"Well, that was fun," she said when we were back outside the tent. We watched a threshing machine clank along.

"Your tits were taking up all the oxygen."

"My tits—" she said, appraising herself—"belong on Mount Rushmore."

And that would have been that. The girl would have been slimly decanted from fat reality, made her way into various anthologies, and that would have been an end to it. Except that six years later I saw her again. Saw her in a reprise of that first time as if reality had cribbed from my poem—the checked tablecloth, the antiquarian sunshine, the chuffing machinery in the background—

I was back at the Workshop, this time as teacher, Judith long gone, lithium/valproate succeeded by Tegretol, which was succeeded by Cibalith-S. I had been through some tough stuff, including a couple of hospitalizations, during one of which I fell in love with this anorexic girl. This was at Mass General, on a ward called Bullfinch 7 where they put the schizos and the self-harming bipolars and the teenage girls with one foot in the grave. We were quite a crew, sitting around the dayroom, half of us talking to the ficus plants and the other half looking like they'd just flown in from Dachau. I was in a manic phase, taking twenty showers a day, and this girl—her name was Lydia—she was trying to get rid of her body. We were a pair. We'd go into her room, close the door against the rules, and she'd say my name over and over—Ichabod Sick, she'd say, like she was tasting the words, Ichabod *Sick*—and she'd describe herself, name each body part like an inventory of disgust, as though what I was doing to her was a punishment, one more way of mortifying her body. Her pelvic bones stuck out like faucets. *Frangible*, I whispered to her like a sex word. She died two months after I was released.

So I was out there at Iowa just trying to hold myself together, keeping my distance from the grad students who wanted to drink beer with the Semi-Famous Young Poet, watching *Love Connection* in my room, or driving for hours through the dirt roads that cut the Iowa countryside. Sometimes I got out and walked through the cornfields, locked myself into a row and just walked, the stalks of corn like blinds on either side of me, and forward the only direction. It was during one of these excursions that I happened upon Steam Days again.

What had been so striking about her as a twelve-year-old— the simple beauty, the asexuality that was so pure that it tipped over into sexuality—was still there in the eighteen-year-old. Or at least the poet Ichabod Sick, standing off to the side in lithium-soaked wonder, fancied he saw in her the marriage of essence and existence, the pure Mennonite spirit poured into the vessel of a lovely young woman. "N-32," a voice called over the PA system. I went up to their table and smiled like a pilgrim.

"Hello," I said.

"Hello," the daughter answered.

"Do you remember me?"

She threw a look at her mother, smiled to try to cover what she must have considered the rudeness of not remembering me.

"Your name is Grace," I said.

"Yes . . . "

"I wrote a poem about you."

At which mother and daughter again exchanged looks. "B-8" the PA announced.

And then I did one of my idiot-savant things. I reached out and touched her. With my fingertips I touched the girl just where her hair swept under her cap. In another second I think the mother would have screamed bloody murder, but I started reciting "The Atmosphere Cleaves," and the sound of a poem suddenly in the air—with its music and illogic, like the English language had suffered a mental breakdown—stopped her. They waited until I was done—until the poem with its liquid eroticism and spangled angels, its bingo game running in the background, had appeared and vanished—and then the mother inserted her forearm in the space between her daughter and me.

"You should go along now."

"Did you like it?" I asked.

"Yes, but you should go."

"I didn't understand it," the girl said. Her mother shot her a look as if to say who cares whether we understood it, you little fool, but the girl kept her eyes fixed on me.

"Who are you?" she said.

I just stood there and smiled—dumb, discovered, outed.

"Martin," I said. The old word felt funny in my mouth. "My name is Martin Browne. Marty."

———

There is about Herman Yoder the stink of life. His thighs get hairy disappearing into his boxers. His toenails are bent and yellow. There is a brown haze of testosterone and semen hanging about him.

Under his yearbook photo it says Nickname: "Yo!" Quote: "See ya, suckers!" Somewhere in the fields, closing in on us, there's the sound of that harvester still.

"Yo," I say. He takes one of his hands out from under his thighs, gives me the finger, and then shoves his hand back under his leg. "You don't understand the position on the board," I say and wave the gun in front of my face like there's maybe a fly bothering me. "No one knows I'm here. There's no traceable motive."

He does a good job of hiding his fear behind the big man's bravado. "You gonna tell her how I cried and begged for mercy? Is that it?"

"What?"

"That pot-smoking bitch!"

"Please," I say. I close my eyes. Through my clothes I can feel *Action Comics* #187 in my back pocket. On page twelve is Superman's dream of a clarified world: a Fortress of Solitude in the arctic waste, without germ, pulse, or decay.

"Tell her to go fuck herself!"

So I shoot his cat. I point the gun first at Herman Yoder's face and then slide it to where Herman Yoder's ugly yellow cat is walking with its slinky haunches and I shoot it. It's a necessary demonstration. A visual aid. The cat flies apart from the impact, then reassembles, rolls over, hisses at the air, tries to get away from its own insides, and then lies down panting. There's surprisingly little blood.

Herman Yoder is screaming. "Skunk!" he cries. "Skunk!"

What kind of human being names his cat Skunk?

"Skunk!"

"You're a very ugly man, Herman Yoder."

He starts to curse me again, but his voice is gone. Over the sofa there's a sign, a molded plastic bas-relief of a handgun with the legend WE DON'T CALL 911. That's as good as a poem.

"Now," I say in a tone of voice that says we understand the position on the board now, don't we? "I'm going to ask you some questions."

He turns a distraught face on me.

"First question." I pause to get my thoughts in order. "If," I say, "the members of the Justice League of America were to inform you that you were to be executed for a crime you had committed, what crime would come to mind?"

He doesn't answer.

"What secret offense from your past proportionate to the punishment?"

It seems to be sinking in. The situation he's in. He seems to be getting it.

"We posit a moral universe in this question," I say. "Things add up. Crime and punishment." And I draw an equals sign in the air with the barrel of the Special.

———

It is to the defendant's credit, Your Honor, that he did not attempt to seduce the girl, to touch her, to force himself on her in any way. He simply wanted to live within the circumference of her spirit. To hear her voice and see her face. That is not stalking; it's breathing

It began quietly. I kept a discreet distance behind the school bus, following it out into the country along the two-lane roads, the snowy landscape broken into forty-acre grids, the stubble of cornstalks under the melting white and the moraine of dirt on either side of the road. I followed her to and from school, sometimes to the library, to the mall with her girlfriends, twice into Iowa City where she went with her mother into the University of Iowa Medical Center. After a week the boys in the back of the bus began to catch on, waving and giving me the finger out the back window. How long it took for her to figure it out I don't know, but by the time I started attending the Lower Deer Creek Mennonite Church—sitting well away from her, mind, but catching glimpses between the lumpen heads and shoulders—I could tell by the way her family sat stiff and self-conscious that they knew.

And then there was a period of a couple of weeks when she didn't go to school, didn't attend church. The pastor during Sharing and Announcements asked for prayers for her, for Grace Albrecht to recover from her affliction, and I was still sane enough to worry that she had fallen ill, mad enough to exult that it was Ichabod Sick they sought to save her from.

In *Action Comics* #187 there's a panel of Superman standing under a shower, only it's not a regular shower, it's a super-blowtorch shower and he's burning off the dirt and stains of the world from his invulnerable suit. This is in his Fortress of Solitude. It's made out of ice. He stands with his legs wide apart and powerful.

When one of the church elders approached me, asked me who I was, that's what I told him. I told him about the super-blowtorch shower. And the cleanliness. And the dirt.

———

On the floor between us, Skunk has finished expiring. I have just asked Herman Yoder if he has some electric clippers, and failing that, a pair of good scissors.

"Your hair," I tell him, wagging the Special like an index finger at his mullet, his body, his whole being. "It's giving off a sour odor."

He gives his head a shake.

"Your body, too."

He just eyes me.

"Undress," I say. "We need to clean you up."

———

The prayers of the congregation worked. After ten days away she was back home, then back in school, back attending church. The poet Ichabod Sick increased his attentions.

Her house was one of those isolated farmhouses you see in the Midwest, with the long dirt drive that right angles through a cornfield up to a simple yard and a plain white frame house. Each afternoon she would step off the bus, empty the mailbox, pointedly not look at the black Pontiac idling at the side of the road, and then ascend the drive, the hem of her long skirt eddying about her ankles, her coat plain—everything about her gray, brown, dull blue—and her clunky shoes and hair swept under her hat, and the poet Ichabod Sick's heart stinging under the super-blowtorch of the sight of her.

When I was away from her, there was the mire of the world all around me, the infection that reached me even out on the frozen plains.

I followed her into Wal-Mart, into Susan's Fabrics. Always at a discreet distance. In the town library with her girlfriends she read *People* magazine under the buzzing lights at the back of the periodical room. When she saw me peering at her through the stacks, she dropped the magazine, hurried and found her friends. They whispered and pointed with their eyes.

At church her father came up and told me to stop it, just stop this, he said. She's just a girl, he said. We'll call the police, he said.

In the hospital it was a gastroenterologist she was seeing, a pediatric gastroenterologist. The digestive organs. Colitis, ulcers, colon cancer—the bacteria raging, coliforms, fecal streptococci.

And all the time I was writing furious brilliant poems about Beatrice and Lana Lane, about the Sons of Levi and the fire that cleanses, poems that later in the hospital, mired in swales of depression, I would find to be breathless and incoherent, ugly on the page with their ill-formed limbs and microcephalic heads.

———

"Grace Albrecht?" Herman Yoder says. He fixes me with a look from behind the soap and the rivulets of blood oozing down his forehead from where he's cut himself. "What about her?"

There is something inexpressibly ugly about Herman Yoder's body. With its massive penis hanging between his legs like an elephant trunk. And the tufts of hair illegibly distributed. The lumpiness about the shoulders, the hirsute back, the thick waist with its red zigzags from the elastic in his boxers.

We have not stopped with cutting off his mullet, but have determined to cleanse his entire body of hair. Accordingly, we have ordered him into his bathtub, and given him his razor and told him to start shaving. First his head, and then his arms, and then his legs, and finally his crotch. The bathwater is turning pink from where he has nicked himself. He has started blubbering once or twice, just like they do in the movies. Once or twice started cursing and calling me names. We have had to discharge a third round into the mirror above the sink by way of persuasion.

Also, the bathroom floor has flooded from where I tried to flush the Achy-Breaky T-shirt down the toilet.

"Did you know her?" I ask.

"She's dead," he said.

"That wasn't the question."

He scrapes the soap from his face. "Of course I knew her. We all knew her."

"We?" I prod. He names his wife, some other names I'm supposed to recognize. He is still convinced that I am here to avenge a domestic squabble. I'm the guy his pot-smoking wife is seeing or something.

"Listen," I say to Herman Yoder. I close my eyes because the shattered mirror is reflecting things I know are not there. "Forget your wife. Your wife doesn't enter into the question. Try to concentrate and answer me: When in the presence of the Innocents, does Herman Yoder do what he can to save them, or does he partake of the massacre?"

He stops shaving his thigh, blinks at me.

"Finds another way home, or not?"

"What are you talking about?"

"Grace Albrecht," I say. "I'm talking about Grace Albrecht."

"I haven't seen Grace Albrecht since high school," Herman Yoder says; then, like enough is enough: "C'mon, man!"

In the state of Iowa "Stalking in the Fourth Degree" is unwanted behavior constituted of, but not limited to, following, telephoning, or initiating communication or contact with a person so as to cause material harm to the mental or emotional health of said person, and is a Class B Misdemeanor.

I was arrested, arraigned, released.

A week later I was arrested again. Two sheriffs showed up at the tent I had pitched on the frozen front yard, rousted me out of my Sub Kilo sleeping bag, cuffed me in full view of the Albrecht family picture window, and drove me to the University of Iowa Hospital where I was held in a locked ward awaiting a competency hearing. The records from my previous hospitalizations were entered as evidence. My sister had to come and testify. And the director of the Writers' Workshop. And then it was back to the locked ward where the manic break happened and I went plunging down into the mire. The walls moved in, the grotto reappeared, I lay flat and two-dimensional on my hospital bed. The spring semester began without me.

In the crescendos of these episodes my memory gets unreliable, but what I think I remember from those last days in the tent is not sleeping and not eating so as not to have to evacuate waste, and rewriting the *Paradiso* by the light of a can of Sterno, and the cleansing cold, and telling Grace as she came up the drive of the plans I was making, me in my smiling madness clutching Superman's Fortress of Solitude in one mitten and telling her as she hurried away about the arctic desolation, about the ice and the stainless steel cold—how we would live with no food, no waste, no tinge of color.

After a month they moved me out of the locked ward and I began the slow crawl upward, like one of those grade-school graphics on the creation of life: the piscine creature humping itself out of the primordial slime, the nubby fins growing into lizard legs, the starter-kit mammal, the monkey puzzled by its tail, and finally the hunched but erect-walking Ichabod Sick.

———

I have asked Herman Yoder for his last words. He is standing in the bathtub with the hairy bathwater lapping at his ankles, a ring of hairy scum about his middle, and his flaccid penis looking like a hanged man.

"The sum of what you've learned in your thirty years. That sort of thing."

I parade him back into the living room, tell him to say goodbye to the pictures on the wall, his mother and father, his kids, the wife I'm sleeping with. And it's here he loses it. Starts to blubber and cry over his kids, Janie and Buddy for god's sake. And he starts to apologize to his wife, says he's sorry, turns to me, his face all blotchy from the tears and the shaving job, and starts to apologize to me, too, says he's sorry for whatever it is, whatever he's done, until I tell him to shut up—just shut the fuck up, Herman Yoder and say goodbye to your kids. He makes a stumbling lunge at me, all blubbery and uncoordinated so that it's an easy thing to dodge him as he sails past. He ends up on the floor, on his hands and knees, crying into the carpet.

"Skunk," he says at the sight of his dead cat, and then like a cri de coeur, "Skunk!"

Somewhere there's a tornado siren going off but it's a balmy October day so maybe there isn't a tornado siren going off. I kick Herman Yoder and tell him to stand up, march him through the kitchen and out into the backyard. There's a stupid Jack'n'Jill well and the corn seven feet tall on three sides and growling unseen in it somewhere the harvester guaranteed to appeal to a poet's fancy. I tell him to enter the corn. "What?" he says and I stick the barrel of the Special right in his naked back and push him toward the cornfield.

"We're going to find the Grim Reaper," I say and someone starts laughing.

When the weather warmed and I had made it back to being half-human, some of the Workshop students began coming to the hospital for tutorials. We met in the sunroom. They brought me flowers, cards, Jujubes because of that poem I wrote about movie theater candy. I was only thirty-two but I shuffled about the corridors in my pajamas like I was seventy-two. My hair stuck out like Einstein's. I affected a grandfatherly German accent, sucking on my Jujubes and offering suggestions to their poems, a bland word changed here, a stale image there, and let's calm down the overactive lineation, ja?

"Like zees," I would say, drawing a line through a word while a young poetess sat next to me with her breasts like frankincense and myrrh, "and zees, ja?"

I lay around my room reading Boethius, took part in group, set off on shuffling hikes through the hospital. I went from ward to ward, through clinics, up to the closed doors that led to the ICU, checked out this sunroom, that sunroom, stared out the front doors at the brightly colored world outside. In the pediatric oncology ward I'd sit in the waiting area like a strung-out parent while wispy-headed gnomes tried to play like normal kids. I got down on the floor and played with them—trucks, Legos, Candyland—shared my Jujubes, and whenever the door that led to the examining rooms swung open made loud steam-shovel noises to cover the sound of crying children.

Sometimes I just sat there like a lobotomized Lepke, missing all the connections.

But my medication was adjusted, adjusted again, and the world began to fit itself back together. My roommate thought it was hilarious that I was a poet. His name was Foster and I called him John Foster Dulles for no reason at all and we watched ESPN together and played Go Fish! and I Doubt It! He was a big guy, farted a lot, which made the delicate red scars on his wrists seem all wrong. When I got tired of cards I'd take to the hallways, bringing the hundreds of pages of my winter mania with me. I'd sit in one of the sunrooms and read through them like they were tablets of cuneiform, looking for a comprehensible image, a salvageable line. I would jot these down in a fresh notebook, maybe start playing with the seed of a poem. During one of these sessions my lawyer called with the news that the Albrecht family had asked that the charges be dropped. The air began to lighten. A poem about the three magi looking for another way home so as not to have to tell Herod about the Christ child began to stumble toward its themes. Advent. Childhood. Destruction. I was working on it—hospital bed cranked up into a reclining position, reading glasses on—trying to rewrite the first line of the second stanza, something about where I had misplaced myself, when Fat Nettie the Nurse came to tell me I had visitors.

"Shoo, fly," I said.

She turned and headed back down the hall, her enormous rear-end square and flat like the back of a snow shovel. In the bed next over, behind the privacy curtain, John Foster Dulles farted.

"*I lost him out behind second base,*" I tried out, "*my sane self, I mean.*"

I let the line hang in the air a moment, then unplugged "*him,*" and stuck in "*Marty.*" Tried that out. Then unplugged "*Marty*" and stuck "*him*" back in. I listened for the zones of radiation, for the breeze from right field. It took me a good minute to realize someone was in the doorway again. And that it wasn't Fat Nettie come back to plump my pillows, or some student, or one of the neighboring nutcases about to call me John Wilkes Booth—

She was in a wheelchair and so changed that even with my reading glasses fumbled off I don't think I would have recognized her if her mother hadn't been standing behind her. Her mother with her mouth pursed, hair up under her cap, body in rigid disapprobation as if she'd lost some argument just minutes before and was here under protest. It was the girl's face that was so different. The clarity was gone—the perfect bone structure I had caressed in the ether of madness—and in its place some illness or medication had painted her features on a ball of dough. Everything was swollen, puffy, and there was a wash of acne across her cheeks and gray crescents under her eyes. But she was smiling, friendly, maybe a little shy at being so bold.

"Hello," she said.

"Hi," I answered like I was fifteen again and couldn't talk to girls. She wheeled her chair a little further into the room. She was in a green bathrobe with fuzzy slippers on her feet. On her lap there was a stack of what looked like music, those old, yellow Schirmer piano editions.

"We were very glad to hear you were feeling better."

"Yes," I managed, "thank you."

"We saw you the other day," she added by way of explanation, "in the sunroom. The one with the piano. I hope you don't mind."

I shook my head "no." I could think of nothing else to say except to ask what was wrong with her, what had happened to her lovely face. But of course I couldn't ask that. One of my legs began to quiver under the covers. "I'm sorry," I said in a shaky voice.

"Please . . . "

"I'm sorry," I said again, and then it was out of me. I sat up in bed, and with my voice all wrong told her I was sorry over and over again. "Steady as she goes, Mr. Sick," I heard John Foster Dulles say from the other side of the curtain, but I couldn't help myself. I kept saying how sorry I was for everything, for frightening her, for hurting her and her family—

"It's all right," the girl was trying to say. "You were ill. You weren't yourself."

"Yes," I said, then in a whisper: "no."

"We don't mean to upset you," the mother said. "Grace just wanted—" She stopped herself. "They told us you were better."

"Yes," I answered. I tried to smile. I tried to look grateful. I tried to look better. "I *am* better," I said. "I just feel very bad about it all. I'm sorry, I can't—" I held my hands out, helpless. "I can't explain it."

"You just gave us a scare," the girl said with a little smile. "But it's all right now. We understand."

I closed my eyes. "Thank you," I said and this deep, deep sigh came out of me. I looked down into my lap, shoulders slumping, face slack like maybe I *had* had a lobotomy. There was my poem about the three magi.

"Well . . . " the mother murmured.

"You know I have a no-contact order on me," I said after a moment. I looked at the girl's ruined face, then up at her mother. "But stay a minute," I said. "It'll be all right."

They remained where they were. But now there was nothing to say. I ended up apologizing for that too. And then I told them if they didn't mind I'd read them the poem I was working on. It was a mess, I said, but it was—and then I said this fancy-pants poet-thing: it was the only myrrh I had. They smiled politely, not knowing quite what to make of that. I slipped my reading glasses on.

And so there in a hospital room in Iowa City, with a suicidal fat farter and a manic-depressive with a salvation complex, and a young woman and her mother just trying to be decent, Herod massacred the innocents again, and the living skeletons on Bullfinch 7 made their bodies disappear, and Marty Browne lost himself out behind second base. Smell of leather, glint of gold, something something something, and a game of *Sorry!* in the kids' oncology ward.

I don't think they made heads or tails of it, but when I was done, the girl said it was lovely anyway. I thanked her, made the usual excuses about it just being a first draft, then laid the notebook aside and took my reading glasses off. Now it was my turn to be embarrassed. I nodded at the piano music on her lap. Did she play?

"Oh, I used to."

"We should be going," the mother said.

"I used to but I quit," the girl went on. "I'm just trying to get a little of it back." She let her fingers dance across a keyboard. "A little each day if I feel strong enough."

"Good," I said. "That's good."

She seemed to understand that I just wanted to have a normal conversation. That it was *important* to have a normal conversation. *She's kind,* I thought, something that had never occurred to me in all my obsessing about her.

"I quit because of a *traumatic experience,*" she said. She turned to her mother. "You remember that?"

"Yes," the mother answered. Noncommittal, like okay we've done our good deed—

"I was in this talent show," the girl went on, turning back to me. "In middle school." And she started in on a story about how she'd messed up in front of the whole school, how she'd had to stop and start over again—this too-hard Bach invention she'd foolishly chosen—how she couldn't see the music because her eyes were swimming, and the outside of me was listening to her, smiling and listening, but the inside was thinking how close to the truth Ichabod Sick had been. Without even knowing it, in his madness, how close to the truth: she *was* something special. It wasn't just empty beauty. She had—hadn't she? in spite of everything?—sought out Ichabod Sick. She had come into his sickroom, into his sick life, and without ever saying it, she had forgiven him.

"I was practically in tears," she was saying. "When I finally finished there's this kid from my class in the wings, and he's holding these tennis balls because he's on next, and he says:

You stink." And she laughed a rueful laugh. "You stink," she said. "This kid. Herman Yoder. I'll never forget it." And she looked down into her lap, at the piano music, at the memory.

"Tennis balls?" I found myself saying.

"He juggled."

"Oh."

And that was it. We said a few more things—I mentioned something about Robert Frost not being able to read his poem at Kennedy's inauguration because the wind made his eyes water—and then she was saying again how glad she was I was feeling better, and I was thanking her, and then with all three of us smiling her mother wheeled her out of the room. A week later I was discharged, and a couple of months after that I left Iowa City. I never saw her again.

But some years later at a posh reception I cornered this miniskirted gastroenterologist and under the ruse of researching a poem asked her about the swollen face, the acne—what GI disease was that a symptom of? No disease, she said, running a finger along her spaghetti straps—medication. Prednisone. Likely prescribed for Crohn's disease, she said—a very nasty condition where the body tries to reject its own intestines, current research indicating that an overactive immunological system was attacking waste in the intestines, usually leading to ulcers, fistulas, a probable colostomy and bowel cancer down the road, did I want to come up and see her medical books sometime?

"Reject its own intestines?" I repeated.

"Too pure for sure," she said. "You can use that in your poem."

Against the wall of corn Herman Yoder looks like an erect, hairless, man-sized possum, all pink and ugly and rodentlike.

"What pleasure in the world?" I'm saying to him. "What small beauties?" We have been cataloging his many murders while the sun shines and the world ripens. I have in my head that October day ten years ago when to keep myself from going mad I hiked through a cornfield not so far from this one and stumbled on Steam Days the second time—the cuts and scratches, the dirt, the smell, and then the beautiful young woman. And now Herman Yoder's skin all red and blotchy from the cornstalks. He keeps asking what the fuck we're doing and I keep telling him that I am annihilating him. I am annihilating you, Herman Yoder, I say and I march him this way and that, sometimes with the corn rows, sometimes against. On occasion the roar of the harvester descends upon us like we're in a fifties sci-fi dinosaur thriller.

"What are we *doing*?" Herman Yoder screams back at me.

"We're looking for sanctuary," I tell him. "The atmosphere cleaving and revealing the untouched breast. N-42."

And I start to call out bingo numbers as we go. Herman Yoder keeps saying that he didn't do anything—I didn't *do* anything, man, he says over and over.

"G-51!" I cry.

"I don't even *know* you!"

"B-8!"

He tries to run—angry, impotent. He crashes through the rows of corn, but he's naked and his feet are bare and hurting and it's no problem for me to keep up. I pelt his glabrous back with bingo numbers. After a couple of minutes we break out into a waste of stubble and dirt. And there's the harvester a few acres away, green and yellow and toylike, a sail on the horizon for poor Herman Yoder who begins running toward it, waving and crying out. It's then that I have to tell him to stop. I fire off a round over his head for punctuation.

"Now, now," I scold when I draw up to him. He is breathing heavily and there are smudges of blood on his shaved legs. He's bent over and he's got his hands on his knees like an exhausted sprinter.

"It's a beautiful autumn day, Herman Yoder," I tell him. And it is. The sky is blue and the sun is shining and there are lovely threads of high cirrus overhead. There are golden and scarlet treetops in the distance and the white steeple of the Historic Register church a couple hundred yards away. These are the sights that surrounded her all her life. This is her home. "This is her home," I say out loud with deep satisfaction. "What?" I hear, but I am closing my eyes, imagining her in the world again—the soft scent of her in the breeze, the deep delicious reds of her jellies, the launderer's soap, the refiner's fire.

"In my travels, Herman Yoder," I say, still with my eyes closed, still smelling the breeze, "I have often thought of Grace Albrecht back here, the fixed point of the compass—" and here I lift my nose to a faint scent of the past—"and whatever happened to me it was all right because I knew that she was here and that it was right that Ichabod Sick should be an attractor of the ugly and the dirty, the sex and the vanity and the petty crimes. It was a way of sacrificing myself."

I open my eyes. He has straightened up, but it isn't easy to stand naked out of doors. Some intuitive shame takes hold of us, doesn't it?—has taken hold of Herman Yoder so he's got one of his arms folded in front of him, his fist tucked up under his chin like a shivering child just out of his bath, and the other hand across his private parts. I put the muzzle of the Special to my lips and kiss it. I'm feeling pretty good right now. The harvester is coming toward us, mowing the circles of hell around us—the dirt, the waste, the remnant stubble—and that feels pretty good too.

"What I didn't reckon on was you back here, near her, you with your tennis balls and the pus oozing out."

The guy inside the harvester has been watching us for some time now. A naked man and a man with a gun standing in the middle of his cornfield! I raise the gun, stiff-arm it at Herman Yoder's head so it looks like I'm about to execute him. Like that famous Saigon photo. The guy in the harvester slides the window back and shouts something at us but we can't hear him over the distance and the roar of the dinosaurs. I calmly swivel the gun, move my arm ninety degrees until the gun is pointing straight at the harvester, straight into the window where the guy starts having a fit. Then I bend my arm at the elbow, bring the muzzle slowly up to my own head and rest it on my temple. I trust all three of us appreciate the tripartite structure, the classical composition.

"I will now recite a poem, Herman Yoder," I say. "It will explain, perhaps, the necessity of our execution."

A pheasant flushes in front of the harvester. The farmer guy is still watching us, twisted around in his seat. He has what looks like a cell phone clapped to his ear. But Herman Yoder isn't watching. He's begun backing up, edging toward the rows of corn, eye on the gun still pointed at the madman's head. He has the look of the desperado who's about to make a break for it. For some reason there's a bell ringing in the cornfield. The average age for onset of bipolar disorder is nineteen.

"*Where then is the other way?*" I start. And there he goes, spinning around like a running back and crashing into the wall of corn. "*Where the world with no Herod and his scimitars?*" I shout after him. I reload my gun, let him think he's maybe getting away, and then tumble into the corn after him. I shout the next line of the poem at his back, and the next, the stuff about the leukemia kid and Lydia with her pelvic bones like faucets. I get out of breath pretty fast, so that by the time the poem peels off into the smell of my Spaulding glove, I'm only pelting him with bits and pieces of it—the sane world of my childhood, a smiling kid, leadoff hitter for his Little League team, and all that goldengrove unleaving stuff. I fire a shot in the air just for the heck of it. And then its on to the fourth stanza with its gift rescinded and the pain and the mania and the crumbling. Babies thrown down wells, skewered on swords. The magi circle back on themselves, return to the manger because there is no other road, there is no other way home. Ahead of me Herman Yoder staggers out of the corn onto a lawn. For a moment I think we've circled back to his house—symmetry!—but then there's a scream. I've got just enough time to see the steeple looming over us—big and white and square—before I'm out of the corn too. There's the little white church I'd passed two hours earlier, and the old graveyard beside it, and out along the road shiny cars and pickup trucks. It's a wedding, for Christ's sake. There's a couple dozen people down along the road and lining the sidewalk running up to the church. The men are all in black. The woman are bright yellow and ruby and lavender. There are some Mennonites sprinkled among them. Some of them are wearing hats like it's 1958.

"And what use?" I shout at them. Herman Yoder has stumbled, collapsed onto the old turf of the graveyard. "This frankincense, this myrrh!"

They turn their eyes from the naked man to the man shouting at them. Who knows, maybe it's a funeral. I lift my arm in the air and the sight of a gun sets everyone running. I fire a round in the air. Ronnie told me it was a weapon, not a gun.

Herman Yoder is saying something. I take a step toward him, bend over his naked body. "What?" I ask him.

"Go away," he manages in between heaves of breathing. "Just go the fuck away."

"Poem's not done," I tell him. I take a step back and catch my breath. There are people hiding behind tree trunks. Behind cars. Other cars are peeling out down the road. There's a little girl in a pretty aquamarine dress calling for her mother. I start in on the last stanza, the stuff about the maculate world and Grace Albrecht's laugh like a necklace of syllables. And with each line I shoot something. I shoot a gravestone. I shoot a tree. I shoot a window in the church so that the glass shatters and tinkles down onto the pews inside. There's screaming and cowering and sudden silences. Some guy who was reaching for a shotgun in the back of his pickup truck has changed his mind and hit the dirt. I reload. I've run out of poem but there's still plenty to shoot. The cornfield. The steeple. A sparrow on a power line. Overhead there's the blue sky all peaceful and untroubled as if there's nothing going on down here. I raise the gun up over my head and take a shot at it. Somewhere there's a child crying. I aim at the sky and take a second shot, a third, but it's still there, still blue and lovely and serene. It stretches from horizon to horizon. And there's only so much ammunition.

Moral Problem #8:
THE ISLAND OF THE FIFTH WHEELS

For the purposes of this next moral problem you may choose your identity from among the population of the Island of the Fifth Wheels. Particular favorites include:

- Gummo Marx, the funniest of the Marx Brothers, who left the act during its vaudeville days to become a haberdasher;
- the original Darren from "Bewitched";
- Pete Best, the drummer John, Paul, and George dumped just before recording "Love Me, Do";
- Piltdown Man;
- the universe that might have occurred 10^{-1} seconds after the Big Bang;
- Saturn, Jove, Ra, Quetzalcoatl, Astarte, and many, many others. Ready?

You are of the almost.

Here on your metaphysical island you sit in the tropical sun, sipping a mai-tai with a plastic umbrella in it, musing, catnapping, wondering by what algorithm of history you are of the false, the forged, the hoaxed, the has-been. The island itself was formerly the set for *Gilligan's Island* but now it has been built up to handle the tourist trade. There are hotels and a Cineplex, an airstrip, bars and bodegas, cabanas lining the lagoon where

Ginger and the Professor used to meet. The tourists fly in on package tours. They like to come and look at you. The real do. The sight of you reassures them, gives them a sense of authenticity, of solidity. It's money well spent.

Today, in the morning paper, in the café talk and the street-corner greetings, there is a rumor of an escapee from the mainland. These runaways are becoming more and more frequent and you wonder why. Last month it was Galileo; the month before Sigmund Freud. What is there about the false that arouses interest? Conversely, what is there about the real that repels? You find yourself growing a bit petulant. After all, if the real is inadequate then where, indeed, *are* we?

Search parties are being formed. You have nothing else to do so you tag along. A little ahead of you is your friend Dorcas. She looks like her name sounds, short, a little fat. She was raised from the dead in Acts 9:40–42 and yet no one's ever heard of her, she says. It's Lazarus this and Lazarus that, she says. She has a snakewood cane with which she beats the bush.

The search takes you to parts of the island never seen on *Gilligan's Island*. The central grasslands and the mountains beyond. You overhear snatches of conversation in Powhaten and Yiddish, in other dead and murdered languages. Somewhere a wag is speaking Esperanto. You get a little sleepy, a little bone-weary and begin to lag behind. The sound of voices grows more infrequent until there is only the baying of the bloodhounds drifting over the tall grass. Then that, too, ceases. The afternoon deepens. You find yourself following a freshet upwards toward the mountains. There is the hum of insects. You move through the miraculous air as if through a dream.

When you find her she is asleep. She is lying on the ground under a banyan tree, exhausted. Her clothes are rent and her hair is a mess but you recognize her. You don't even need the giveaway of the dusty halo. You know her from the pictures, the images, medals, icons, the hundreds of Annunciations,

Pietàs, the Madonna-and-Childs, the nativity scenes in terracotta, wood, bronze, marble, plaster, plastic, cardboard. How
in her single face she can radiate the multiplicity of her imagined selves is a question that does not even occur to you. It is
just the magic of the island. You are used to it. But here's what
you must decide:

Do you turn her in or not? Do you hand her over to the real or
offer her asylum here among the unreal? It is a difficult and en-
gaging question. You will need to contemplate whether she has
merely run from her responsibilities or whether some deeper af-
firmation is at work. If so, what might that be? Is there an integrity
to illusion after all? Something to be cherished in the false, in the
alternate, in the dream that supersedes the real?

You sit on a rock and begin scratching equations in the dirt.
It may take you some time to figure this one out.

THE LAW OF MIRACLES
or, Five Ways My Wife Could Die

When the tree fell on my house, I was already on my way down. Wife gone, son gone, middle age just around the corner. There had been no hurricane, no stiff in-line winds: the tree just fell over—plunk! The rafters snapped, the window imploded, and there I was lying in bed going eenie-meenie-minie-moe as to whether it would be Seconal and scotch or a razor in the bathtub.

In probability theory we have an axiom called Littlewood's Law of Miracles. The Law of Miracles is based upon a paradoxical feature of chance, *viz.* that given sufficiently large numbers, unlikely events will happen unexpectedly often. (Hand me that piece of chalk.) If we define a miracle (M) as something that happens once in a million events, and take as a given that we see and hear such events (e) at a rate of about one per second (boy on his bike, sun coming out, Toyota approaching), then since we experience roughly a million such events in a month of waking life, by the laws of probability we should experience a miracle about once a month. The uncanny isn't uncanny after all. Jesus just happened to hit with Lazarus. The scotch is supposed to exacerbate the effect of the Seconal.

I didn't used to be depressed. I used to be a happy man. I had my wife. I had my son. I had my job with the New Jersey Gaming Commission. I had a house in Stone Harbor a block from the ocean that was appreciating 28 percent a year. For years my wife and I had managed to fend off the real estate developers while the cottages up and down our street were torn down and replaced with postmodern mansions. But after the tree fell over, the developers renewed their suit. They could smell the injury, see the depression leaking out of the little house. They offered me a cool million. I explained to each the Law of Miracles, the flow chart of coincidence that had brought me to where I was. The woman from Coldwell Banker upped the offer to a million, one.

It began raining in my bedroom. The occasional swallow flew in, perched above my dresser, and then flew out. The tree, I explained to the paperboy, was an environmental improbability. The coastal soil was too shallow, too sandy. It should never have grown where it did. Never reached the size it did. A delegation of my neighbors dropped by—friendly, smiling millionaires asking if they could help. It'd been over a week now, they said, did I want the tree service called? They understood how difficult things were for me—would I again accept their condolences?—but the neighborhood was at risk, its appeal was seriously impaired and really, we didn't want the lawyers to get involved, did we?

On the back porch, my son's baseball cleats lay where he'd kicked them off ten months earlier.

It was not unusual for me, lying in bed, to see through the broken branches and the wilting leaves, airplanes trolling the beach with their advertising banners, parasailors arcing across the blue. These were events. One per second. Other events included Discontinuation of Service notices from South Jersey Gas, peanut butter and tequila the only food in the house, me standing on my front lawn explaining to the police in their squad car that no, no I wasn't planning on removing the tree, and why? well, that was a good question.

At work I was on probation because of some bad attendance patterns dating back to when Peggy left me. I didn't know whether I cared or not. If I killed myself then pfft, but if I didn't then I needed a job, didn't I? Anyway I'd been sort of demoted and was back to testing randomly seized video slots for compliance with Commission regulations, looking for anomalous code, algorithms that defeated the random. Which is tricky because it's an axiom of probability theory that any equation that appears to generate randomness cannot be truly random. It makes you wonder about the universe itself, whether behind the seemingly arbitrary there isn't a massively complex equation in charge, so baroque in its calculation of every cell division, every breath, bird, and bagel, that we can only see in it chance or luck or fate. Things are either random or they're not. There is no in between. This is what I tell my estranged wife—my lovely, dear, irreplaceable Peggy—when she falls out of the sky into the hole in my roof.

"Meant for each other," I tell her while her exhausted chute flaps in the wind. Her face is scratched from the tree branches. Later, in the emergency room, they'll discover a cracked vertebra, a broken rib or two. But right now, she just stares at me through the impossible leaves.

Go ahead, you can look it up. You can Google it: keywords <Stone Harbor parasail accident>. You'll get news stories from the *Cape May Star*, the *Philadelphia Inquirer*. And there's the WPVI Action News story including video footage from the boat as the tow line snaps and the bright indigo canopy luffs and then floats off across the sky, heading toward the beach, toward the housetops behind, growing smaller and smaller while whoever's holding the camera back on the boat (Peggy's boyfriend, if you must know) keeps saying "oh man oh man oh man." She misses the mansion to the right of us, the mansion to the left, gets hauled up one side of our roof, dragged down the other until she snags in the branches that seem, she will say later, to be growing out of the roof, not in. When she comes to a stop she finds herself staring into her old bedroom.

Good for me then, that I haven't changed a thing.

The cell that goes wrong first—is it like that kid you remember in the fourth grade? The one who just can't get anything right? Who just seems born wrong, except now he's going to show them, boy! the other cells, the cells who do their homework on time, who sit forward in their seats, who don't talk, get a hall pass when they need to go to the lavatory . . .

The symptoms first appeared when Peggy was pregnant with Aaron. She found herself getting tired easily, having trouble breathing. For a time it was a subject of some humor in our household—was this really fit Peggy McFarland, the gal who used her second serve when she played tennis with her husband?—but then in addition to the weariness and the breathing, her right eyelid began to droop. Her puzzled obstetrician had some tests run on her but they all came back negative. We were on the verge of phoning New Jersey Neurological with a referral when—as if it had made a mistake, wound up in the wrong body—whatever-it-was put its hat back on, packed its suitcase, and left. Peggy's strength returned, her eyelid quit acting weird, she creamed me 6–2, 6–1. Three months later she gave birth to a 7 lb. 7 oz. baby boy—no painkillers, thank you very much. But inside her, an oddball cell in her thymus divided in two.

It was six years later at a game of tee-ball—Aaron at second base, proud parents in the bleachers—that I noticed the eyelid was drooping again.

It was six years later when she pulled the binoculars away from her face—we were birding down along Hereford Inlet—that I noticed the eyelid was drooping again.

It was six years later after we'd made quick, secret love—Henrietta Pussycat babysitting Aaron in the next room—that I turned my wife's flushed face to me and noticed the eyelid was drooping again.

This time it got diagnosed correctly. Autoimmune myasthenia gravis—a muscle disease in which a meddlesome immune system mistakenly attacks itself. It is rarely fatal, the neurologist informed us with a smile. In many cases it cures itself, he said. Or goes into deep remission, as it apparently did in Peggy for six years. It was increasingly treatable with immunosuppressive drugs. The major concern was if the thymus was involved, and they would want to test for that.

The probabilities were as follows:

⇛ incidence of myasthenia gravis in the general population— .012%

⇛ and within that population, incidence of thymoma— 11%

⇛ and within that population, incidence of malignant thymoma— 12%

⇛ and within that population, incidence of invasive malignant thymoma— 18%

⇛ and within that population, incidence of death— 100%

which yielded the following equation:

PROBABILITY OF PEGGY'S DEATH =
$(.00012)(.11)(.12)(.18)1$
or
.000000285
or
3 in ten million

which meant, when she died eighteen months later, a week before Aaron's eighth birthday, her death fell well within the parameters of a miracle.

———

To hell with 911. How often in life do you get to rescue your wife?

I get out the extension ladder from the garage, climb up on the roof singing the Mighty Mouse song, get the harness unhitched from the canopy chute, then the canopy chute unsnagged from the tree branches so the wind carries it off the roof. By the time the Emergency Rescue Squadron pulls up in their lime-green vehicle, I'm kissing my wife all up and down the side of her face, her neck, on the scar where a benign thymoma was removed six years ago in a transcervical thymectomy. She's telling me to quit it, 'cause it's making her laugh, and jeez! her ribs hurt. Blind to the poetry of the moment, the rescue guys slide my ladder out of the way, erect their own in its place, climb up the roof and tell me to stand clear. It takes them five minutes to extricate Peggy, strap her onto this lightweight stretcher they've got and rappel her toward the lawn. On the way down she says "Guys, is this really necessary?" then waves to me as they hustle her across the front yard. They slide her in the back of the emergency vehicle and speed off with the siren doing its war whoop.

For the first time I look through the hole in my roof from the outside, see my side of the bed where I've laid for so many years, the empty other side, the bottle of Seconal on the nightstand beside my pillow.

———

That Friday in June when Peggy was driving Aaron home from Little League, only one factor in the spinning wind, in the dot-and-dash of the traffic, needed to be changed for tragedy to pass over my wife and son as though the roof of their car were marked with lamb's blood.

My boy was a second baseman. Second base is the position that the medium kid plays. The kid who is medium-good, medium-quick, medium-coordinated. He doesn't have the arm the shortstop has, isn't speedy like the centerfielder, but neither is he retarded like the kid who gets stuck in right field. It's the perfect position for a regular kid whose normalcy seems like a freak of nature to his father. It wasn't Little League but the grocery store they were driving home from.

They were driving home from the orthodontist's. They'd skipped lunch because they'd had to drive from the middle school over to Swainton, where Dr. Williams had his office, and now they were hungry. They had pulled into KFC (which no longer meant Kentucky Fried Chicken as it had in my childhood but had become a meaningless abbreviation, and if that fast-food organization had not dissolved the relationship between substance and symbol, would my wife still be alive?) and so had an open bucket of chicken balanced on the emergency brake as they approached Stone Harbor Bridge, to hell with teaching the kid road safety, Margaret.

Have the factors all taken their places? The platinum shiver of the sun on the bay water below, the two-way traffic, the bell-curve of the bridge, the innocent catamaran with its indigo sail passing underneath?

But she didn't die from the accident. It wasn't the accident that killed her. She died of suffocation. She died because Aaron was acting goofy in his seat, imitating King Friday the 13th and Henrietta Pussycat, and Peggy was laughing because that's what you're supposed to do when your child is socially at risk and you don't want to humiliate him because he isn't actually being funny at all, but you laugh and the piece of chicken in your mouth gets sucked down into what your grandmother used to call your Sunday pipe, and you can't quite believe it won't come unstuck, any minute now it's going to come unstuck, and then at the edges of your shrinking vision there's an SUV crossing the center divider or no, it's you who's crossing the divider, and the last thing you hear is your son screaming "Mom!"

If I haven't already intimated it, my wife is a tough cookie.

Three days after the parasail accident she's up on the roof with a rented chainsaw, handing down branch after branch to where I'm standing on the lawn below. She's got on this sports bra thing that doesn't quite cover the bandage on her ribcage. I shout over the chainsaw for her to be careful. She hands down another limb with the suggestion that I start a curbside pile because Frank is swinging by later in his pickup.

"Who's Frank?" I ask.

"Frank," she says. "You know Frank." She guns the chainsaw.

I do not know Frank. He is an integer from outside my set. There may be others.

But she's here. And not just because she still owns half the house and a hole in her investment can't be a good thing. I watch her stride atop the roof, watch her toss her hair out of the way when she sets herself over a limb, watch the tendons behind her knees, the knuckles of her shoulder blades. It bears repeating: That's my wife up there. Ever since she moved out ten months ago she's been going haywire with life, with windsurfing and parasailing and jetskiing Franks. It has been her way of coping. But now she's come home. With each limb she lops off, the air grows lighter.

When she's done, when she's cut everything back so the only thing left is the bole of the tree with its mass of upended roots, and there's a pile of branches out beside the street and a face cord of firewood against the side of the garage, she holds her naked arms out to me like whew! is she filthy or what? So five minutes later I'm standing outside the shower, eyes averted, a bath towel draped over one arm, and over the other a pair of culottes she left behind when she moved out, and a Margaritaville tanktop we'd bought down in Key West a dozen winters ago. She opens the shower door a crack, lifts the towel off my arm, pulls the door shut again. A minute later when she steps out she's got the towel wrapped around her torso in that way only women know how to do. And her red hair has gone all corkscrewy the way it does.

We make a pitcher of margaritas with a packet of bad margarita mix left over from some party in some other life. When we make love I try to be careful of her ribs.

———

What the grand jury determined was this: on June 19, 2002, Margaret Lydia McFarland went into an Atlantic City liquor store after work; an armed robber came in after her; she attempted to intervene in the robbery; she was shot; the gunman fled. She did not know her assailant, nor did her assailant know her. It was an event (e).

A Mr. and Mrs. Donald Arquette of Wilkes-Barre, Pennsylvania, filed a deposition testifying that earlier that day they had been present at the deceased's place of business, the Tropicana Hotel and Casino, when the deceased received a phone call. A bottle of tequila was mentioned. A meeting time. The deceased was a redhead.

Was the telephone call from the deceased's husband? The deceased's husband testified no.

The deceased's husband also testified that his wife trailed would-be lovers like a dog in heat: men whose wives called the house looking for them, sad lesbians who lingered on the fringes of their parties. Her allure, the deceased's husband testified, was a function of her being. It was the (f) of P, he said, and like all the others the murderer—for the moment, ladies and gentlemen of the jury, let us call him Frank—misunderstood that. He thought the warmth of the deceased's smile, the wet syllables of her laugh, meant something. They did mean something, the deceased's husband testified, just not what the would-be lovers thought they meant.

Did she recognize him in those last seconds before her abdomen was ripped open? Under the pantyhose mask, whoever he was: Frank, Fran, Franklin? In that last second before the laughter trembling on her lips was stopped by the bright bark of the gun?

According to the store clerks' testimony, she collapsed backwards against a shelf of vodka, slumped to the floor. Some bottles tumbled down and broke. One of the clerks stepped forward and not knowing what else to say, asked her if she was all right. The other gave her a roll of Viva, stepped helplessly back. She started to soak up the puddle of vodka under her, then understood and held the roll of paper towels to her gut instead. Perhaps she marveled at Frank, at the planning, at the ingenuity of the seemingly random camouflaging his sitting in the parking lot waiting to see if his calculation would hold up—that of all the liquor stores in Atlantic City it was this one she'd most likely pass on the way to his house. And now here she was, sitting in a puddle of vodka, dying. "We called 911, lady," one of the clerks kept saying until the other clerk told him to shut up. After five minutes the vodka began to turn pink. And then something funny was happening to her eyes. Something was leaving. Something was going away. She tried to lift her head to see what it was but she couldn't. Somewhere there was the sound of a siren, but then that, too, went away. And then she remembered her husband.

She remembered him making a siren sound. (One of the clerks testified that she laughed just before she died, a bubble of blood attaching itself to her lips.) They were in college and she was lying on someone's dorm bed. A party was going on and she was passing a joint to the guy lying next to her, holding it to his lips and her husband, only he wasn't her husband then, he was just a college guy she hardly knew, a math major sitting on the floor across the way and every time she touched this guy who was lying next to her, this math major made a siren sound—*whoop! whoop! whoop!*—a silly stoned thing to do that made everybody laugh. Only he wasn't fooling *her*, she knew he was jealous, she knew it because of the way he looked at her, the way he watched her, and what he'd said earlier, that thing about how she was all innuendo, and when she'd laughed and acted insulted, how he said he'd elaborate if she would like, that it wasn't anything she *said*, it was how she looked, it was her body, her *body* was all innuendo. And that was when she thought she might like him to touch her. Only he wouldn't because he thought she was trouble, a big flirt he said. And it was only when he saw her making out with Clarence at the dean's house that he began to understand, coming back from downtown with ice-cream cones, spring semester of their senior year, and Clarence bounding up to the fence with his tail wagging, and her kneeling down, letting that gorgeous Irish setter lick her ice cream between the pickets, and then her face, cooing and baby-talking the whole time, and the math major holding back like *good grief*, until she stood up with a smile and for the first time took his arm as they walked, and a few feet further down the sidewalk, she turned back to Clarence and threw the dog a look the man beside her must have recognized, a look of intimacy, like she was saying *we, we two, us redheads, we're both alive* And then he began to understand. He began to appreciate her.

———

In Psalm 46 of the King James version of the Old Testament, which appeared the year Shakespeare turned 46, the 46th word from the beginning is "shake" and the 46th word from the end is "spear."

It surrounds us like magic—the humdrum miraculous.

We've got the bed pulled out into the middle of the room so that we are right under the hole in the roof, right under the purple blaze of the Milky Way. Peggy's head is on my pillow. My head is on Peggy's pillow. The Seconal has been slipped into the nightstand drawer.

She has finished crying now. The room is filled with the ghostly ruin of her sobbing. It has been ten months.

We have each of us been saved so many times. The missed

connections, the space between the landmines. Raise your glasses, Mr. and Mrs. Donald Arquette, and drink with me to the does-not-equal sign: to the cell that didn't divide, to the SUV that didn't cross the center divider, to all the incomplete equations that reside at the back of the universe like unmatched socks in our sock drawers.

Let us say, then, about that day I walked downtown for ice cream with that pretty, flirtatious psych major—what was her name? Peggy something?—anyway that girl I knew in college, let us say that instead of walking past the dean's house on the way back to campus, we turned down Spring Street and entered a different universe where there was no Clarence waiting for us, no subsequent kiss behind the fieldhouse. And let us say (if it will help save the thirty-eight-year-old woman lying next to me, the woman who has begun crying again, softly, to herself), that she became someone else's wife and I became someone else's husband—perhaps yours, or *yours*—so that in this universe it's *our* son who is bicycling home from soccer that day ten months ago, his sun-kissed hair like a proof of God, and it's *you*, not Peggy, who is working in the yard when you hear the squeal of tires and then the tin-can rattle and smash, and when you reach our beautiful boy his grass-stained shin guards are up around his knees from where he has skated across the pavement, and the blood is leaking quietly from his head, and the front tire of his bicycle is spinning like a roulette wheel on some millionaire's new-mowed lawn.

Moral Problem #9:
A COSMIC DIVERTISSEMENT

You are the Creator. It is 1.8^7 seconds after the Big Bang and everything is going swimmingly. The other universe that could have happened at 10^{-1} seconds didn't, in fact, happen (as You knew it wouldn't) and You are in the first microseconds of being distributed through time and space. Electrons and positrons are zipping about annihilating one another. Every few minutes, just as a *divertissement*, You double in size. In a little while it'll be every million years. At the tips of Your fingers and toes the first galaxies are beginning to form, and You are already looking forward to the details: stars, planets, life. It's twelve billion years away but what the heck, You're in no hurry. You've been through this before—expansion and contraction, bang and crunch—only this time, on some out-of-the-way planet, how about a race of ethical beings, someone to keep You company in the interstellar dark, not like the last universe with its clockwork animalism, its amoral squids—*pah!* all that instinct!

You lean back and stretch Your toes, sip Your cosmic daiquiri. You can hardly wait. This is going to be a good one. This is going to be fun.

ACKNOWLEDGMENTS

"Hands" and "The Madonna of the Relics" originally appeared in *The Kenyon Review*; the individual "Problem" pieces originally appeared consecutively as "A Few Moral Problems You Might Like to Ponder, of a Winter's Evening, in Front of the Fire, with a Cat on Your Lap" in *The New England Review*, as did "Being and Nothingness (Not a Real Title)"; "Missing, Believed Wiped," first appeared in *The Massachusetts Review*; "Presently in Ruins" in *StoryQuarterly* and *The Pushcart Prizes*; and "The Law of Miracles" in *Fiction* under its original title, "Five Ways My Wife Could Die."

In writing the "Moral Problem" pieces, I had to step well out of my own personal experience, and I would like to acknowledge here some of the books that helped me do that: Feng Jicai's *Voices from the Whirlwind*; Henry Munson Jr.'s *The House of Si Abd Allah*; Sam Driver's *Anna Akhmatova*; and Harrison E. Salisbury's *The 900 Days*.

JUNIPER
PRIZE
FOR FICTION

This volume is the sixth recipient of the
Juniper Prize for Fiction, established in 2004
by the University of Massachusetts Press
in collaboration with the UMass Amherst
MFA Program for Poets and Writers, to be
presented annually for an outstanding work
of literary fiction. Like its sister award, the
Juniper Prize for Poetry established in 1976,
the prize is named in honor of Robert Francis
(1901–1987), who lived for many years at Fort
Juniper, Amherst, Massachusetts.

Fic Smit   1119733 $19.95

Minnesota Book Award Winner